"The Legend of Match" © 2018 Pam McCutcheon
"Stuck with Santa" © 2018 Angel Smits
"Mistletoe Kisses" © 2018 Pam McCutcheon
"The Sugar Cookie Miracle" © 2018 Jodi Anderson
"A Christmas Catch" © 2018 Karen Fox
"A Letter to Santa" © 2018 Jude Willhoff
"A Perfect Christmas" © 2018 Sharon Silva
"Operation: Christmas Surprise" © 2018 Laura Hayden

ISBN: 978-1-941528-86-0

Parker Hayden Media
5740 N. Carefree Circle, Ste 120-1
Colorado Springs, CO 80922

Art credits:
Cover Design: LB Hayden
Legs: tawanlubfah/DepositPhotos
Dog: mdorottya/DepositPhotos

A DOGWOOD CHRISTMAS

A DOGWOOD SWEET ROMANCE ANTHOLOGY

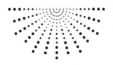

JODI ANDERSON   KAREN FOX   LAURA HAYDEN

PAM MCCUTCHEON   SHARON SILVA

ANGEL SMITS   JUDE WILLHOFF

PARKER
HAYDEN
MEDIA

THE LEGEND OF MATCH

For those unfamiliar with the series, here's how Dogwood's famous matchmaking dog came to be....

THE TOWN of Dogwood was settled southwest of Colorado Springs during the 1860s by the Blakes and McPhersons, miners wanting to exploit the mineral deposits in the area. The McPhersons brought some of their beloved dogwood trees with them, and in this area, the most temperate climate of Colorado, they found the perfect spot to plant them down by the river. The trees thrived, giving the town and the creek their names.

One fine Memorial Day a few years after the second world war, the story goes that a group of young men were building picnic tables and gazebos by Dogwood Creek so that everyone could enjoy the beautiful area in comfort. The young women of the town pitched in with food and drink to reward the young men and, subsequently, use the new park for the first time. As the young ladies waited for their beaus to finish, they wove garlands and crowns from the fallen pink blossoms.

One young woman named Susannah had brought her dog with her—a black Labrador retriever puppy with a curious heart-shaped blaze of white on his chest. She'd been training him to carry messages between her and her beau, Robert, so when the young men completed their labor, Susannah jokingly tossed her crown of flowers around her dog's neck and bade him carry the token to her one true love.

The puppy cocked his head and stared at her for a moment as if seriously considering her request, then unerringly made a beeline for the young men. Susannah laughed, wondering how Robert would react, but the dog dropped her offering at the feet of a shy young man named Johnny who had been admiring her from afar. Emboldened by the dog's choice, Johnny stared at Susannah with his heart in his eyes and she knew, all at once, the dog had chosen the perfect man for her.

No one remembers what the dog's name was up to that point, but since he had brought two unsuspecting soul mates together, he became known as the matchmaking dog, or Match, and the name stuck. People brought their hopes of a similar union to Match, and he took his job seriously, pairing couples who belonged together, and refusing to confirm matches that wouldn't work. He was never wrong, and Susannah and Johnny lived a long, love-filled life together.

After a rich life of bringing couples together, Match eventually crossed the Rainbow Bridge, and a beagle puppy with a brown heart-shaped marking was born in Dogwood. It soon became evident that the puppy possessed the same ability to see into lovers' hearts, so she was named Match as well.

After each Match passes on, a new Match is born in Dogwood. The dogs' breed, color, and gender have varied widely over the years, but each has a heart-shaped mark located somewhere on their body, proudly proclaiming their ability and responsibility to bring soul mates together.

STUCK WITH SANTA

BY ANGEL SMITS

NICK KEENE HADN'T WANTED to take this job. But wanting was one thing, and his mother was another. She wasn't administrator of Dogwood Memorial Hospital because she was a pushover—that was one thing she'd *never* been. Only his dad had been able to get her to loosen up a little.

Now that Dad was gone—and this was the first holiday season without him—Nick felt like he should give her a little extra attention.

Which totally did not explain why he was standing here, waiting for the elevator to reach its destination, wearing a Santa suit.

Okay, half a Santa suit. The blasted thing was hotter than heck, and he'd done what he could to cool off once he'd escaped the three dozen kids at the hospital's party. His hat was in one hand, and the big red coat hung open to let in some air. The pillow his mother had stuffed under the loose coat was in his other hand.

Right now, he just wanted to get to his car and grab his gym bag where he kept his workout clothes. Cooler. Comfortable. Normal.

With each floor he passed, there was a dinging sound, and the sign overhead changed from one number to the next. The building only had eight floors, so it shouldn't take long to get to the garage.

Except the thing kept stopping. On the fourth floor, the elevator stopped—again—and the doors slid open. He cringed. *Please don't let some kid be out there or get on.* That'd be a real wake-up call. And Mom would have a conniption fit.

Thankfully, there weren't any kids on the other side of the door. He breathed a sigh of relief—and nearly choked. No kids.

Worse.

Holly Buchannon stood there, her eyes wide, her arms full of odd-looking equipment. Rubber shapes and forms. A bent plastic tube. She had a full load and, over the pile, she stared at him. Her eyes were wide and such a deep blue—even bluer than he remembered.

"Hey," he said over the tightness in his throat. He could tell she was seriously thinking about taking the stairs. He stepped all the way to the back of the elevator. "Come on. I won't bite." Much.

Now why did he have to say that? Why did he have to remember that one night?

She completely ignored his comment. "You really think it's a good idea to run around dressed like that?" She frowned at him as she stepped inside, and the doors slid closed.

"Like Santa?" He looked down. "Fits the season."

"No, like a half-dressed, fake Santa," she snapped. "What if some kid sees you?"

Why did she have to think the same thing he had? They'd always been like that, though. "I was being careful. You ever wear one of these things?"

"Uh, no." Holly turned around, putting her back to him and ignoring him.

He couldn't ignore her. She was right there. So close. So familiar. Her dark hair was pulled up, just like always when she worked. She claimed it kept the curls out of her face while she worked with her physical therapy patients. She didn't want to cut it, so all those lovely curls were wound into a tight bun on top of her head.

Leaving her neck bare. Nick stared at the soft, pale skin there—and remembered more than he should. He cleared his throat, hoping to dislodge the memories and longing he couldn't seem to escape.

"Did you say something?" She glanced over her shoulder.

"No, just clearing my throat." He scooted back farther, leaning against the rail on the back wall.

"You're not getting sick, are you?"

"No. Just the heat."

"It's only ten degrees."

"Outside. In here, it's hotter than..."

"Ah, ah, ah. Santa doesn't curse."

She was enjoying this. *Damn it.* Then, as he stood there another minute, he chuckled. He was enjoying it, too. He'd missed the fun they'd had. Missed the friendship he'd had with her—before they'd made the mistake of stepping beyond friendship.

A sudden jolt nearly sent him to the floor. And the armload of junk she held—or had been holding—dropped all around them. She cursed softly, and he couldn't help but laugh. Apparently, *she* was allowed to use colorful language.

"Wh...what happened?" Holly looked back at him.

"I don't know." He wasn't sure, but he had an idea. "I think we're stuck. We're not moving." Frowning, Nick stepped over some foam rubber squares, dropping his hat and pillow into the mess. He pushed a couple of the round buttons on the panel. Nothing. They didn't even light up. Next, he pulled open the little door that held the emergency phone and picked up the old-fashioned handset. He waited for someone to answer.

🐾 🐾 🐾 🐾

HOLLY WAS FAIRLY certain Santa was not supposed to have six-pack abs. From the instant she'd stepped onto the elevator, Holly had known this was a mistake.

But it was too late now. Santa SixPack was here to stay. And so was she.

She couldn't help wondering how Nick's mother had managed to con him into playing Santa. Even when they'd been getting along, and she'd hoped their relationship would grow into something more than friendship, she'd known that wasn't his kind of thing.

"Hello? Anyone there?" His voice, familiar and oh-so-sexy, filled the tiny space. How many nights had she fallen asleep with his voice weaving through her mind? KDGW, the local radio station, had made their best decision in hiring him.

Late-night DJ with a deep, nerve-soothing voice and slow smooth jazz...

"That you, Del?" Nick's voice wasn't calm now as he talked to the head security guard, Delbert Hines. "It's not moving. Yeah." Nick looked up at the number strip over the doors. "Looks like between three and four, but I can't be sure."

He listened again, then sighed. "Sure. We'll do that." Nick glanced over his shoulder at her. "No, I'm not alone. Holly Buchannan from PT is here, too."

The silence in the elevator made it easy to hear Del's voice, but Holly couldn't quite make out the words. She tried and then gave up. What did she need to know anyway?

"Sure. Thanks." Nick gave the man his cell phone number

and then put the phone back into its neat little box. He turned around slowly. "Well, looks like we might as well get comfy. We're gonna be here a while."

Holly's heart sank. She'd been on her way to see her last patient for the day. She'd had a full schedule since early this morning. She was tired. "I don't have time for this!"

Nick laughed, and the warm sound shivered over her. "The repair crew has to come from Colorado Springs." An hour away, at least. "And to be honest, I'd rather wait than have good ol' Del or Phil in maintenance try to fix it."

Okay, he had a point there. Everyone in the hospital loved Del and Phil. But no one was under any delusion that they were cutting-edge. Not working at Dogwood Memorial. Nice guys, but—

"Yeah." She sighed. "Guess we might as well make ourselves comfortable." She shoved the equipment scattered on the floor into a pile with her foot and scooted down to sit, trying really hard not to think about all the things on the floor she was sitting on.

Nick did the same on the opposite wall. His Santa jacket fell open, showing her again the solid chest she remembered—

No, do not go there. Holly tore her gaze away, though not without noting the way the red velvet pants and heavy black boots fit him. On anyone else, they'd have looked silly. On him? She swallowed the dryness in her throat.

Focus on something else. Anything else. It was, after all, the Christmas season—as his attire attested. She had plenty to think about and do.

Holly hadn't ever really cared for this time of year. When she'd been a kid, her name had been a favorite taunt of her classmates. Her favorite holiday, if anyone asked, was Halloween.

She vaguely remembered asking her mother why she'd

given her that name. Mom had simply laughed, never really answering.

Setting those thoughts aside, Holly watched Nick as he leaned against the back wall of the elevator, one long leg stretched out, the other knee lifted, his wrist resting on top. He leaned his head back, and his eyes were closed. Was he sleeping? He had to be exhausted. He'd worked last night.

Heat warmed her cheeks, and even while she knew his eyes were closed, she looked away from him. He was too good at reading her. So what if she still listened to his show every night? It wasn't like Dogwood was Denver or even Colorado Springs where there was a myriad of radio stations to choose from. Here, there were only a couple. And she liked jazz.

And his deep, late-night voice.

"What's got you blushing?"

That voice cut through her every fantasy. Surprised, she looked up at his smile, then hastily back down again. "I'm not blushing." She fanned herself. "It's warm in here."

"Yeah." He leaned his head back again and closed his eyes. "December isn't exactly time to run the air conditioning." He sighed.

"I doubt it works in here, anyway. Not when nothing else does."

"Good point." He smiled.

They sat in silence for a bit. She couldn't hear any activity beyond the wide metal doors. "Who do you think is out there?"

"Depends if Mom knows or not." He looked at her then. "Even if they all know, if she's out there, they'll scatter. She's probably terrorizing everyone."

"Yeah. She's kinda good at that." As soon as the words were out of her mouth, she wanted to clap her hand over her errant lips.

But his laughter made her rethink that. "Hey, I grew up living with her, remember? There's a reason why she's a great administrator." He paused. "Or drill sergeant," he mumbled.

This time, Holly laughed, but managed to keep her mouth shut. The silence that fell between them wasn't as uncomfortable as before. She relaxed. And for the first time since this stupid elevator had gotten stuck, she drew an easy breath.

❅❅❅❅

NICK LEANED back against the wall of the elevator, stretching his legs out. Since he was over six feet tall, the small space was not the most comfortable place he'd ever sat. Holly sat opposite him, her much shorter legs barely reaching the halfway point.

"How'd your mother rope you into the Santa gig?" she asked.

He looked at Holly, feeling safe in taking in the view since her head was tilted back and her eyes were closed.

"How does she get anything? Guilt. She's a pro at it."

Holly laughed. "Yeah, she is. You should have seen her last year at the fundraiser dinner. No one left without putting money in the pot."

"I can see that. This year, she wants me to emcee the thing."

Holly didn't say anything at first. She did nod. Then she surprised him by lifting her head and looking straight at him. "You'd be good at it."

"That's what she said."

She laughed again, but didn't say anything more. The silence stretched out, but he didn't feel uncomfortable. He liked it. He'd always been comfortable around Holly. That comfort had been what spooked him.

From that first day, he'd liked Holly. Liked talking with her, and not just about music, though that was enjoyable. No, other topics as well. They hadn't always agreed, but it hadn't really mattered.

"Why don't you want to do it?"

"I didn't say that."

"You didn't have to. I can tell you don't want to."

"How?" She intrigued him, and to be honest, she bothered him. She'd always been able to read him, to know almost before he spoke, what he was going to say. After just a few days of spending time with him, she'd been able to finish his sentences.

She'd intrigued him—and scared him.

"How what?"

"How can you tell I don't want to do it?"

"Your expression, for one. Your frown deepened when you told me she wants you to emcee."

"It did?" He hadn't realized it.

"Yeah. And your body language is total refusal. Stiff shoulders. Crossed arms."

He mentally cursed—and uncrossed his arms. Her soft laugh sounded so good.

"How do you know all this?" Reluctant to open up any more, he was intrigued by her ability. It was almost like a superpower. Curious, he leaned forward and looked closer at her.

"What are you doing?" she asked.

"Trying to figure *you* out."

"Give up." She waved a hand at him, dismissing him, with a smile.

"No. I'm curious."

She gave him a look he couldn't decipher. Dang, how did

she do that? Turn him inside out.

He'd never met anyone like her, before or since that afternoon they'd met at the summer picnic last year. After college, and a stint on a small LA radio station, he'd decided to move to Dogwood, following his parents here from the West Coast. His mother had been intent on introducing him—and showing him off—to the town.

And he'd met Holly. He couldn't remember a single other soul from that day, though he'd met several. As he'd settled into his new job and place, they'd become friends. Good friends who spent the summer casually going out with her friends and sometimes his coworkers.

Until the whole group had gone out dancing for someone's birthday. He couldn't even remember whose birthday, but he remembered that first kiss.

This time, he did feel the frown that formed on his brow.

"Didn't you ever take any psych classes in school?" she asked, saving him from his own thoughts.

He thought back. "Yeah." School was ten years ago. "Not that I remember a thing."

"I guess it's because I work with people all day long. There's so much to learn and observe. And if I can't at least make an educated guess of what they're thinking, I won't be successful treating them."

"Don't they tell you?"

She laughed, and it wasn't a happy sound. "People are never honest."

Her voice dipped with her disappointment. What was she disappointed in? Him? Life? People?

"They hide their pain, they refuse therapy, they pretend they're fine when they aren't." She looked at him then, and he didn't have to be an expert in people, like she was, to read that one. He was definitely on that list of people she was disappointed in. He sighed and stared back. She finally looked away.

Shifting, trying unsuccessfully to get comfortable, he bent his other knee. "Maybe they aren't as aware of themselves as you'd like. Maybe they don't want to be."

"Ah, denial." Her voice faded. "A lovely place to live sometimes." She didn't sound convinced. "I lived there once."

That surprised him. Surprised him quite a bit, actually. He wanted to ask, which also surprised him. He'd never been one to be curious about other people. She stirred up strange feelings and curiosity in him. And he wasn't a total idiot. Something was bothering her.

Question was—did he want to ask? Did he really want to know? He let the silence stretch out, hoping he'd figure out what to say. He almost laughed out loud. He spent most nights in a soundproof room talking to himself for six hours —and now he was at a loss?

Suddenly, something groaned, like metal rubbing against itself. "What's that?" she cried.

"Uh, I don't know." Whatever it was, it didn't sound good. Reaching up, he snagged the emergency phone again. Maybe someone had answers for them.

※ ※ ※ ※

"WELL, tell him to cut it out," Nick snapped and hung up the phone. He looked over at her. "Phil thought he'd pry open the doors on the fourth floor, see if he could help." Nick rolled his eyes. "That was the pry bar on the doors."

"Isn't the repair crew coming?" The idea of anyone getting hurt scared her.

"Yeah. He's impatient." Nick grinned. "Mom's up there yelling at him for scratching the doors."

Nick's mother was technically Holly's boss. As the hospital's administrator, she ran the show. Holly liked her, but the woman was fierce.

Looking at Nick now, she wondered how things were going with him and his mother. Everyone had heard about her husband's sudden death last spring, and while Monica had taken some time off, she'd stayed very much in charge.

"Sorry to hear about your dad," Holly whispered.

He looked up, seeming surprised. "Thanks."

Their eyes met, and she couldn't look away. His brown eyes were as deep and soulful as his voice, and she felt herself getting sucked in....

Nick cleared his throat, breaking the tension and connection.

What was wrong with her? Looking anywhere but at his face, she couldn't help but notice the strands of long white hair on the Santa suit. Searching for a distraction, she picked up the hat that mingled with her equipment. "I see Muffin was with you." The big, loveable therapy dog that belonged to her best friend, Katie, practically lived at the hospital.

"Yeah." Relief washed over his face at the change of subject. "She was with me up until I got on here." He looked around at the elevator. "At the last minute, she turned around. Someone must have called her."

He frowned then. "She nudged my leg like she was saying, go on without me." He laughed. "She's nearly human, I swear."

"Yeah, she is." Holly smiled. The big loveable sheepdog mix had nearly free run of the hospital, and always seemed to know where she was needed, and who needed her most.

"Mom will never admit it, but I'm not sure she'd have recovered from losing Dad without Muffin." His words were soft, and almost hurt to hear.

"She would have." He seemed to need her reassurance. "She's strong. But what about you?" Holly couldn't recall any break that he'd taken from his nightly broadcast. "You didn't take any time off."

Silence fell heavy between them. "You listen to the show?" he asked, softly, sounding almost surprised.

"Of course I do." She leaned against the wall. "You know I like jazz." They'd talked about it for hours...back when they were talking.

"Yeah." He was silent for a long time. "What, no comments? No suggestions of how to improve the show? Everybody else has."

She tilted her head to get a better look at his expression. "That sounded rather bitter. What happened?" He'd been so excited about the job last summer, and his love of the music had been so strong.

"Sorry, guess I'm just tired."

She let the silence stretch out just long enough. "If it helps, I like how you do your show. But that didn't sound like just tired." The fact that he was here, in the middle of the day, probably jacked up his sleep schedule. "That sounded...almost...downtrodden."

He opened one eye. "That's a bit melodramatic, don't you think?"

"Maybe. But I don't know of a better word to describe it. If it's not right, tell me why it isn't."

"I'm not one of your patients, Holly."

"I know that." She looked down, trying to sort through the responses to find one that didn't make her sound mean. She didn't come up with anything, so chose to remain silent.

❖ ❖ ❖ ❖

HE'D NEVER BEEN good at sitting still for long periods of time. Even when he was on the air, he got up and paced a lot. Thank heaven for wireless headphones. He'd upset her when he'd snapped at her earlier, he knew that. He needed to break the uncomfortable silence. "What's all this for?" Nick stared at all the odd physical therapy paraphernalia on the floor around them. Foam shapes, a curved bar, giant rubber bands. All brightly colored and strange-looking.

Holly's face slipped into a sad frown, and he felt a stab in his chest. Whoever, or whatever this was for, she felt emotional about them. "I was on my way to see Mrs. Lawrence."

"Who's she?" he asked softly.

She paused, and he could see that inner struggle he saw on his mother's face whenever a case at the hospital was important to her. When that caring conflicted with all the privacy laws and rules that permeated healthcare. Just like his mom, he knew that Holly needed to talk to someone about the pain he saw in her eyes. He waited. She had to be the one to make the decision.

"She broke her hip a few weeks ago, and she's not..." Holly paused and swallowed hard. Her emotions showed in her eyes and looked like tears. "She's not doing well. I hoped the bright colors, and my going to her room instead of bringing her down to the gym, would help."

"But you didn't get there."

Holly nodded, glancing down and picking up one of the bright tomato-red rubber-band-looking things. She absently pulled it apart, stretching it over and under her leg.

"Are you always this invested in your patients?" He remembered when he'd pulled his shoulder skiing a couple of years ago. That guy had barely paid attention to him. Just gave him exercise lists—while he was on his phone.

"I care about all my patients." Holly lifted her face and looked at him, a bit of indignation on her face.

"I appreciate that." He trod carefully, but knew she needed to share her feelings. "But?" he nudged.

She played with the rubber band a bit more. "Mrs. Lawrence is special." Stretch. Stretch. Stretch. "She was my elementary school principal."

"Ah." He tried to sound like he understood.

"No. You don't understand."

That had definitely hit a nerve. He waited while she fought to control her reaction. He watched. "Then help me understand," he finally said softly.

She didn't look up, like he'd hoped. He liked seeing her eyes. They were so blue, and told him what she was thinking. She continued to absently stretch the band. He wondered if she was counting and actually exercising. He smiled at the notion.

"When I was in fourth grade, my mom died in a car accident." Holly whispered the words, and he felt the stab at his heart. He was twenty-eight, and losing his dad last year had been the worst thing he'd ever experienced.

To be so young and lose such an important person... He and his mother argued, regularly, but he appreciated her—more so now that he'd grown up.

"I'm sorry."

She was silent for a long minute. Was she remembering? Mourning?

"Thanks," she whispered. "It was really hard that year at school. I fell behind because I missed so much time. At Christmas, all the parents came for the programs. Our teachers had us make Valentines and gifts. They had a Mother's Day tea..." Her voice cracked.

"And you didn't have anyone there."

Holly looked up then, and the sight of those beautiful blue eyes drowning in the wet tears made him want to fix everything for her. And he knew he couldn't.

"No. I had Mrs. Lawrence come sit with me. She stood in for my mom." He barely heard her words. But once his brain wrapped around the understanding, he smiled. He definitely wanted to meet the sweet woman who meant so much to Holly.

"She came in to the tea in a pretty dress, just like all the moms were wearing." Holly smiled at the memory. "She usually wore a business suit, but that day, she was a woman. A mom. Not the principal. She'd even let her hair down." She played with the rubber band some more. "I didn't even realize she had long hair until that day. I just..." She shrugged. "After that, she still wore it in an updo—except when we were just us. Then she always let it down." Her voice faded out, and he was fairly certain she was lost in her memories.

"Sounds like a special lady," he whispered, not sure she was ready to leave her own thoughts.

"Yeah." Holly shook her head as if breaking out of her memories. She looked at him then. "That's why I feel like I owe her. I have to help her." The urgency in her voice was tinged with pain. His arms ached to reach out and hold her, comfort her.

Nick's phone rang then, breaking the pained silence and saving him from doing something stupid. He looked at the screen. "It's the guard station."

"Why do you have that number in your phone?"

"How do you think I get in touch with Mom? Hello?" he answered.

Del's voice came on the line. "The repair guys are here. They are heading up to get to work."

"Good."

"Nick." His mother's voice came on the line, and he had a vision of her yanking the receiver out of poor Del's hand.

"Yeah, Mom?" He looked over at Holly who smirked at him. She was holding the Santa hat now, absently playing with the round puff ball on the end—like it was a stress ball or something. Her long fingers curled around it, absently rubbing the soft fur....

"Did you hear what I said?"

"Uh, sorry, Mom. Guess I'm tired." He could have been wide awake and still not heard his mother with Holly right here.

"Well, maybe this is an opportunity for you to take a break." She slipped into her "mom voice" and he smiled. She didn't use it often anymore. "And tell Holly hello for me," she added.

"Will do."

"We got another call coming in, ma'am," he heard Del say.

"'Bye, Mom." Nick ended the call, so she didn't have to. She wasn't very good at saying goodbye. And Del needed to do his job.

"Mom says hi, by the way." Nick hadn't stopped watching Holly, but now that he was off the phone, she looked up at him again—and hastily dropped the Santa hat back to the floor. Her cheeks were tinged a bright pink, and he knew his thoughts were clear in his eyes.

For the first time since he'd told her he wasn't interested in a long-term relationship, he realized what he'd given up. What he'd lost.

🐾🐾🐾

HALF AN HOUR LATER, they were still sitting on the floor of the unmoving elevator car. "Here." Nick pushed the pillow that had doubled as his Santa belly toward her. "You look beat."

"I'm fine."

He laughed. "No, you're not. They aren't going to get us out of here for a while. Take a break." He nudged the pillow again. "Still burning the candle at both ends?"

He knew her too well. "Yeah," she admitted. "And in the middle sometimes." She stifled a yawn and reluctantly snagged the corner of the pillow. "What are you going to do?"

"Sit here and watch you sleep." He winked. "Don't worry about me. Just rest. You look like you could use it."

That was not a compliment, and she knew it hadn't been meant as anything more than encouragement to make her take his offer. Plumping the pillow, she scooted over. The elevator car was wide enough for her to stretch out, and, to be honest, it felt good.

She'd already put in a full shift today. After her last session, she was supposed to meet her best friend, Katie, for dinner. She glanced at her watch. Well, she wasn't going to make that, but at least the odds were Katie already knew Holly wasn't going to make it. Katie was a discharge planner here. She owned Muffin, the therapy dog, and she knew everyone.

Del or Phil would surely tell her.

She spoke her thoughts aloud. "I hope people aren't out there worrying about us."

He didn't respond right away, and she wondered what he was thinking. "I suppose they are. Mom, for sure."

Yeah, Monica Keene was probably driving the repair crew crazy.

"Who—" He cleared his throat. "Who else do you think would be?"

She glanced over at him. He was frowning. "Oh, Katie Day, I'm sure." She watched him nod.

"Anyone else?"

"No." She levered up on an elbow. What was that look on his face? "Nick?" She wasn't even sure what she was going to ask him, but what was he thinking? Was there someone else he wanted to be out there, worrying about him? She tried to wrack her brain for some memory or comment that would give her a clue. Had Monica mentioned something? She frequently talked about her son in casual meetings. Anything he'd hinted at on air?

"Yeah?" The expression on his face told her nothing.

"Who else do you think is out there?"

He shrugged. "No one."

They'd just told each other so much...with only a few words. Neither of them was seeing anyone. Why did a thrill and relief slide through her? Hiding her reaction, she nestled down on the pillow again.

She closed her eyes and willed sleep to take her. It wasn't being cooperative. And she knew why. Admitting it to herself was hard. Admitting it to him—worse. "Nick?"

"Shh, you're sleeping."

She laughed at his bad attempt to joke. "Talk to me," she whispered.

"Ah, at least I have one fan."

"Don't rub it in. You already know I listen. Others do, too."

"Uh-huh."

His soft laugh soothed her. She closed her eyes and settled back to find sleep.

"What exactly am I talking about?"

"I don't know. Anything. How do you come up with things to talk about on the air?"

"Hmmm..."

Silence stretched out, and she thought for a bit that he was going to ignore her request. She'd eventually sleep.

Suddenly, soft music—jazz—whispered around the small space. "It's not my full collection, but it's what I've got down-loaded on my phone," he said, in that soft, late-night voice. Deep and rich, it wafted around her, weaving in and out of her every sense.

"That's Paul Whiteman, the undisputed king of jazz, who was a regular on the airwaves for nearly thirty years. He's always been one of my favorites." The music continued, and Holly felt herself relax. She sighed, and wasn't sure if it was out loud, or not.

A brief silence led into the next piece. His voice grew even deeper. "Close your eyes on this one, folks, and let it reach deep for that spot in your soul. You know, that warm spot you'd love to stay forever.""You should read bedtime stories," she whispered, not opening her eyes, not wanting to as relaxation slipped over her.

"I thought that's what I was doing. Go to sleep, Holly."

Nick watched Holly as she snuggled against his pillow. He knew the instant she fell asleep. Her features relaxed, her hands no longer gripping tight to the pillow. Her lashes were dark against her smooth, pale skin, and her lips parted just enough to tempt and tease him.

He'd missed her. How the hell that had happened, he had no clue. He'd never missed anyone before. Not even his parents, especially not Mom, when he'd gone away to college. But he'd missed Holly countless times since they'd parted ways nearly three months ago.

Settling back, he let himself watch her. This might be his last opportunity to do anything like this.

Oh, they'd managed to admit—indirectly—that neither of them was seeing anyone. He was relieved, but he wasn't a fool. Any chance he might have had with her might have already slipped away. If it hadn't, it was awfully close.

SOMEONE WAS POUNDING ON A DOOR. Holly tried to pull herself out of the dream about being stuck in an elevator, but it wouldn't let go. Wait—

She opened her eyes and saw the ugly carpet of the elevator floor and a pair of boot-clad feet.

It wasn't a dream.

"'Morning, sleepyhead." Nick grinned at her.

"Please tell me it's not really morning." She sat up, shoving the strands of hair that had fallen out of her bun from her eyes.

"Figure of speech." Nick pushed to his feet. His steps were halted, slow.

"Are you okay?" Her therapy eye already told her something was wrong.

"Yeah, just a charley horse in my leg." He cursed as he put his foot down again. "I think I sat too long."

"Why didn't you get up and move around?"

"I didn't want to wake you." He paced the short length of the elevator car and back again. He glanced at her and tried to smile. "It'll ease up in a minute."

"Do you get these often?"

"Sometimes, Dr. Holly," he teased. "I just walk them off."

"Uh-huh." She watched him with a critical eye. "Let me check your leg."

His only response was to lift an eyebrow. She crossed her arms and waited. Not like either of them was going anywhere. Finally, his movements became more fluid, and his steps even.

"Okay." She shoved the pillow toward him. "Lie down. And take off the jacket. You have to be melting in it."

"Now she wants it off," he said to no one in particular. "Make up your mind." With a pained grin, he stripped off the heavy red Santa coat.

"St...stop stalling." She patted the expanse of carpet.

"Come on." She refused to acknowledge the bare chest right there in front of her...but that didn't mean she didn't notice.

Nick reluctantly stretched out on the floor, his head on the pillow where she'd just been lying. She tried not to think about the intimacy of it all, tried to step into the professional persona that kept her mind off him as a person and on his status as a patient. Except he wasn't a patient.

He was Nick.

Clearing her mind, she reached for his thigh. The hard, muscular ridges of his leg made her hands feel small. Slowly, she moved her fingers up and down the length of his thigh, checking for damage and trying to ease his pain. His grunt of reaction told her where the muscle was still tight. "Here?"

"Yeah. Man, that sucks."

"Hold still. Let me do a couple of things." She moved, straddling his leg, doing a deep massage on his entire thigh. He closed his eyes, and a bit of her discomfort faded.

She'd done this hundreds of times before. Athletes were especially prone to problems like this, and they frequently came into the clinic. "Any better?" she asked several minutes later.

Nick nodded, and she could feel his muscles relax. "I can feel it letting go."

She massaged, gently, making sure to hit pressure points. "If you do some stretching exercises regularly, it should keep you from hurting. I'll give you a list."

He opened his eyes then, and his gaze found her. Holly couldn't look away. Her hands were still on his thigh, and the heat in his eyes hit her hard. Time vanished. The world around them, small as it was, faded into the distance. "Nick?" she whispered.

"Holly—" He was closer now. Had he moved? Had she? He reached out, his big palm warm against her cheek. Gently, reverently, he slid his thumb over her lips. "Thank you," he whispered, and the warmth of his breath washed over her.

"No problem." She didn't pull back, simply continued staring into his deep, dark eyes.

"God, I've missed you," Nick whispered as he moved closer to her. His eyes closed, his lips parted.

Leaning toward him, Holly caught herself before she fell against him, her hands splayed against the broad ridges of his bare chest. She could push away. She could stop him.

But she didn't want to. She wanted him. Wanted to feel his arms, taste his kiss, be with him. His words echoed in her head. *I've missed you.* "Me, too," she whispered as she closed the last few inches between them and kissed him.

He tasted familiar, felt warm and safe. Not wanting the moment to end, she leaned in closer.

Just then, the elevator car jerked. The distant sound of machinery kicking to life surrounded them.

Nick didn't push away; neither did she. For a long instant, he held her tight, held on. Finally, she pushed away, just a bit. Just in time to hear the doors slide open.

"Do we have an audience?" he asked softly.

"I'm afraid to look." Her cheeks warmed though.

"Okay, on three, let's look together."

She nodded. "One. Two. Three." They both turned their heads. Yep. An audience.

Nearly a dozen people—and two dogs—stood there staring. Delbert and Phil chuckled first. His mother stood there, her hands on her hips. Katie was there, too. The other therapists from her department stared at her.

And...was that Mrs. Lawrence in the wheelchair? Mortified, Holly buried her face in Nick's shoulder. Breathing in his scent, she nearly forgot where she was.

"I thought Muffin was the only therapy dog here," Nick said.

"She is."

"Uh...who's that?"

Holly lifted her head, and looked again. They both stared at the other dog sitting beside Muffin. The black and white border-collie mix was familiar to nearly everyone in Dogwood. "Match." The matchmaking dog.

"Is she grinning at us?"

"Dogs can't grin," Holly said.

"That one is."

Just then, Match gave a yip, and Muffin tilted her head back and answered with a yip of her own.

"I think that's approval." Nick pushed up to a sitting position and pulled Holly close. "And I wholeheartedly agree."

This time when he kissed her, the applause in the background was loud and clear—and quickly faded into the distance.

MISTLETOE KISSES

BY PAM MCCUTCHEON

Fifteen years ago

"Mo-o-om," Jessica McPherson yelled. "Amber painted the dog!"

Twelve-year-old Amber shot a killing look at her older sister, wishing her eyes really could shoot deadly darts. Why did Jessica have to embarrass her in front of Dillon Hart? *Now he'll never play this game with me again.*

Their mother came in to Amber's room, looking perplexed. "You painted the dog?" She examined the Jack Russell terrier. "Where?"

Jessica pointed accusingly at a spot above Rascal's tail. "There."

"It's only a small spot," Dillon said, giving her mom that big smile that seemed to work on all adults.

Well, at least Mom didn't go ballistic. Instead, she sighed and darted a look at Jessica. "Thank you. You may leave now. I'll take care of this."

Her bratty older sister left, but not before she stuck her tongue out...behind Mom's back, of course.

Mom gave Amber an exasperated look. "Do I need to ask why you painted a heart on Rascal's rear?"

"We were playing a game," Dillon volunteered from the bed. "Rascal was playing Match, Amber's looking for a soul mate, and I'm the photographer capturing it all for paternity." He held up the brand-new digital camera he'd gotten for his birthday, and Rascal yipped in agreement.

Mom's lips quivered. "I think you mean posterity."

"Yeah, that."

"I'm sure you did a good job, but I'd like to talk to Amber alone, please."

"Sure, Mrs. McPherson. See you later, Ammie." Dillon gathered his stuff together, then headed out the door, giving Amber a grimace behind Mom's back. Was that supposed to be support? *Gee, thanks, Dillon.*

Her mom closed the door, and joined Amber on the bed where Rascal jumped up to sit beside her.

"I didn't hurt him," Amber protested. "And I made a heart out of a black spot he already had, so it isn't much paint— and it comes out with water, honest!"

"I see that," Mom said. "But perhaps it wasn't the best idea to paint his fur, even if you did want to pretend he's Match. I just..." She paused, taking a deep breath. "I didn't realize you'd started thinking about boys in that way."

Amber's face heated. "Maybe a little.... You know—I've heard all the stories about how Match brought you and Dad, and Grandma and Grandpa together."

"I see. So you're hoping Match will bring you a soul mate of your own?"

No, duh. Look how happy they all were. Who wouldn't want that? "Yeah."

"And was Dillon playing your soul mate?"

Amber grimaced. "*No.* He's my best friend—he can't be my soul mate. He was playing the *photographer,* to capture my look when I find my soul mate—whoever that is." Amber framed her face with her hands, contorting her face into the expression she'd practiced in the mirror.

Mom's lips quivered again. "I see. You do know that Match will decide if and when you're ready, not you. And it doesn't happen at your age. You're too young."

"I know," Amber said, drooping. "I just want to be ready when it does happen."

Her mom hugged her. "Don't worry—you will be. Now, let's get that paint off Rascal, shall we?" She stood, and Rascal yipped and jumped off the bed.

Amber stood reluctantly, trying not to show her relief. She'd gotten off eas—

"But, Amber?"

Uh-oh. "Yes?"

Mom leveled The Look at her. "No more boys in the bedroom with the door closed."

Amber rolled her eyes. "Mom, it's *Dillon*."

"I know, but still. Them's the rules."

"Whatever," she muttered. Sheesh—like she had to worry about Dillon.

❖ ❖ ❖ ❖

Ten years ago

AMBER STARED LONGINGLY at the kids around the dog fountain in the town square. The popular kids laughed and shoved each other, casting looks over their shoulders to see who was watching them. Everyone, of course.

The only one who didn't look to see who was watching was Tony Duarte, senior class president and major hottie. He didn't need to—he was so totally cool and confident. And he'd never looked twice at her. No guy did—not in the way she wanted, anyway. But she had a lot of good friends who were boys. How the heck could she get out of the Friend Zone?

Dillon nudged her with his elbow. "You mooning over Phony Tony again?"

She glanced at Tony, who was who was letting his retriever mix drink from the fountain, hoping he hadn't heard. "He's not phony," she protested. "He's the only one of them who isn't."

Dillon raised his camera and took a couple of shots of them. "Okay, you have a point. But look at this." He showed her the photo he'd taken of the "in" crowd. "I'll call it 'A Study in Egocentricity.'"

She snorted. "Good one. And I think you actually used that word correctly." He'd gotten better at using big words over the years.

He put his nose up in the air in a show of being haughty. "Of course I did." He ruined it by grinning at her.

"So why are we here again?"

"It's my Photography Club assignment—I'm supposed to take photos of iconic...things around town."

"Things?" Where were his big words now?

"Yeah, you know. Stuff that makes Dogwood so special." He gestured toward the fountain. "And even though it's a silly statue of a peeing dog, it's iconic here."

"Only because it's in the image of the original Match." But the current Match didn't seem to have any interest in finding Amber's soul mate, no matter how many times she'd asked the dog.

"Duh." He framed the shot with his lens. "Plus, the artist wanted to give dogs a place to have a drink during the warmer months."

A thought suddenly came to her. "Well," she said casually, "another reason it's iconic is because people rub the crystal for luck in romance." The heart-shaped stone on his chest was in the same place where the first Match had the marking of his heart, and everyone believed rubbing it would ensure the current Match would find them a soul mate. Heck, it was worth a shot.

"Want me to pose for you, doing that?" she asked. When he gave her a sidelong glance, she added innocently, "What could be more iconic than that?"

He leered at her knowingly. "Yeah, right. You just want an excuse to rub the lucky heart...or get closer to Tony."

He had her there—she'd hoped for both. But she didn't dare admit it. She shrugged.

"But it's a good idea anyway. Go on." He waved her toward the fountain.

Amber approached the fountain, and when she saw one of the girls roll her eyes and deliberately turn her back, her steps faltered. Crystal probably thought Amber was trying to horn in on their group.

Blessedly, Dillon came to her rescue. "Right there," he called out, raising his camera to his eye. "Now touch the heart on the statue, pretend you're wishing for luck."

She cast him a grateful glance—everyone knew that Dillon co-opted anyone and everyone he could for his photographs. She hoped the silly girls were jealous—they always wanted their picture taken, but Amber was his favorite subject. She turned her back on the group and faced the statue.

"Don't look at me," Dillon called out from behind the camera. "Just pretend you're a tourist hoping for love."

She reached out to touch the lucky stone and closed her eyes, making a wish. *Match, please bring me my soul mate.*

"Good, good," Dillon called. "Now lean in and kiss it."

What? She cast him an incredulous glance.

"You know, like the Blarney Stone in Ireland."

The idiots behind her laughed, and then she heard one voice ring out. "He's right," Tony said. "I've seen tourists do that here."

That shut the others up. With Tony's blessing, she closed her eyes, puckered her lips, and leaned in toward the statue.

A sudden wave of water soaked her front and she opened her eyes and mouth in surprise, only to see Tony's enthusiastic retriever jump up to give her an enthusiastic lick...right in her mouth. Yuck! Who wanted to French-kiss a dog?

As she backed away, her shorts and T-shirt soaking wet, the girls cracked up. But they subsided a little when Tony came forward with concern on his face. "Sorry about my dog," he said, gesturing toward the boisterous retriever who was playing happily in the fountain. "He gets excited. I'm sorry you're—" He glanced down at her front, and his face turned bright red. "Uh...wet."

Everyone went quiet, and Dillon inserted himself between them. "I'll take care of her," he said gruffly. He took off his shirt and handed it to her.

"It'll get wet," Amber protested. *Just like me.*

"Yeah, but it's better than—" He gestured awkwardly at her front. "You know."

She looked down at her wet T-shirt. *Oh, no. Flash much?*

She grabbed his shirt and shoved it on quickly. "Get me out of here," she muttered.

"You got it, Ammie." He steered her away from the crowd of gawking spectators, and didn't even care when she sat down, practically squishing, in the front seat of his car.

She beat her head against the dash. "I can't believe that just happened."

"Don't worry about it. I predict you'll be a lot more popular with those guys from now on."

She groaned. Not exactly the kind of attention she

wanted. Especially since touching the statue hadn't brought any luck at all.

Present Day

AMBER LEANED her head on her hand at Sanctuary's counter, playing with the wedding invitation and trying to find a good excuse to decline. Could she come down with the flu? Have an accident? Stage a fight with Bliss and Luke?

She sighed. No, she couldn't do any of those.

Dillon waltzed in, his dark blond hair mussed as usual, with his camera around his neck and a duffle bag in his hand. He gave her a dazzling grin. "So who's on tap for photos today? I hear you got a new batch of dogs in right before Thanksgiving."

"Don't ask me," Amber said bitterly. "Ask Kat."

"Who?"

"Kat Channing. She's the new volunteer coordinator."

He cocked his head at her glum tone. "Why so mopey, Ammie? I thought you wanted someone to help with all the work around here."

"I do. It's not that."

"You don't like her?"

She shrugged. "She's okay, and the animals love her. Plus, she's Lira's new owner, and that has helped Sanctuary out a lot." Using the retired movie star dog to draw attention to the no-kill shelter was a brilliant idea. "That was Mike Duffy's idea."

"But...?" He snapped his fingers. "Oh, I get it. Another potential match went *pfft?*"

She grimaced. He knew her too well. "Yes. Kat just got engaged to Mike."

"The volunteer vet?"

She nodded. "Match brought them together at the Thanksgiving dinner."

"Match has never been wrong...."

She sighed. "I know. But I've tried for so long to get Match to identify my soul mate. Since it hasn't happened, I figured it must be someone from outside Dogwood." Hence her flirtation with Mike, who lived in Colorado Springs. She was embarrassed to remember how she'd thrown herself at him.

"It'll happen when both you and your match are ready—you know that."

"I know, I know." But she wanted it now.

"Maybe Match is having a hard time finding someone good enough," Dillon suggested. He came around the other side of the counter to give her a one-armed hug. "I mean, look at you—kind, beautiful, a great friend..."

She rolled her eyes. "Yeah, everyone's best friend. Yippee." She paused to wave the wedding invitation in his face. "And now this."

He snatched it from her hand and read it. His expression turned puzzled. "You hoped Luke would be your match?"

"No, of course not. That would be gross. He's my cousin." It seemed she was related to half the town, including both founding families—the McPhersons on her father's side, and the Blakes on her mother's. "But I don't have a date for the wedding. Pathetic."

"So don't go."

"I have to. He's my cousin." Of some sort or another.

He shrugged. "No problem. I'll be your date."

She glanced at him in surprise. "You?"

He looked hurt. "What's wrong with me? I clean up well."

She knew that—his popularity with the female half of

Dogwood was a testament to that. "Sorry, that's not what I meant. But everyone knows we're best friends."

"So? Can't friends become soul mates? How will they know we haven't grown into a couple?"

She grimaced at the mental picture of them growing parasitically together like two clinging vines. "No one will believe it—they'll know it's a pity date."

He regarded her silently for a moment. "This is really important to you?"

"Yes, it is." Having a date for the wedding would help her actually enjoy it, instead of fielding questions about her love-less life, and being embarrassed about her flirtation.

"Then let's pretend to be more than friends."

She glanced at him in surprise. "You'd do that for me?"

"For you, of course. I'm not dating anyone at the moment."

"But doesn't your business pick up at this time of year? The wedding is on Christmas Eve." He'd become semi-famous for his fabulous pictures that captured the essence of Dogwood's many pets, and lots of people wanted them for Christmas cards.

He shrugged and grinned again. "Somewhat, but most of them already had their appointments, so they could have prints in time for Christmas mailing. We can have a few very public 'dates'..." he made air quotes with his fingers, "before that so it won't seem so strange."

"Then we'll break up?" she asked doubtfully.

"Sure. We'll just tell everyone it didn't work out, and we're better off as friends. What do you say?"

She glanced at him assessingly. Well, he was fun to be with, so it wouldn't be a hardship, and some people—her family mostly—had been expecting them to get together for years. "Okay, sure. That might work." In fact, it was just the ticket. She hugged him. "You're the best."

Dillon couldn't help but grin. Making his best friend feel better improved his day tremendously. On impulse, he said, "Okay, let's start now and spend time together. I don't need Kat to help me when I have you. Show me the dogs who need photos for the website."

"Awesome."

And now she was back to the cheerful Amber he knew. He followed her back to the pens.

She glanced over her shoulder. "Those pictures you took of the last batch were a huge hit. Most of the dogs were adopted in record time."

And that's why he'd volunteered to do it. Every dog deserved a loving home—cats, rabbits, goats, and other animals too. If he could make them seem more appealing to potential adopters by taking a few photos, it was well worth his time.

He left some of his equipment props here for just that purpose, and busied himself setting up while Amber went to get the dogs. She came back with the first batch and he indulged himself by petting them for a few minutes. He could never resist a furry face, especially those poor dogs who had been abused in the inhumane puppy mills. He felt compelled to show them some humans were kind. "What theme did the volunteers come up with for this batch?"

"They gave them all holiday names, hoping that would make them more adoptable this time of year."

"Great! I brought extra Christmas props for the photographs." He put a red backdrop up, draping it over some boxes, along with fake snow.

"So, who's first?"

She picked up a cute little Jack Russell terrier who reminded her of her childhood pet, Rascal, only he lacked the bounce you normally found in the breed—the puppy mill had probably scared it out of him. "This little guy is Rudolph."

"Perfect!" He pulled out a red nose and a fake set of antlers. Rudolph wasn't too crazy about them, but Dillon distracted him with treats, and got some great shots.

"Okay, who's next?"

They took photos of Holly, Noel, Jingle, Donner, and Blitzen, and he had the perfect props for each one.

"These are great pictures," Amber enthused, and picked up a tiny Yorkshire terrier. "What props do you have for Mistletoe here?"

He put a spring of plastic mistletoe jauntily behind the Yorkie's ear, but it didn't quite work—it was too big for the tiny dog. He thought for a minute, then snapped his fingers. "I know. Come over here in front of the backdrop."

"Why?" she asked in trepidation. "You don't want me in the picture, do you?"

"Why not? You should be used to it by now."

She rolled her eyes, but came closer. "I don't really want another picture of me getting French-kissed by a dog. You'd probably plaster that one all over the internet, too."

Dillon laughed. The picture he'd taken of the dog kissing her at the fountain had won some awards. "No—mistletoe doesn't kiss. Mistletoe *causes* people to kiss." He dragged her over to the backdrop. "Sit here, on the floor. I'll put Mistletoe —the dog—above us."

"Us?"

"Yeah, sure. We'll pretend to kiss below Mistletoe, and it will not only be great for the website, but might get people talking—in the way we want them to."

"How can you take the photos and be in them, too?"

He held up his remote. "With this. Easy. Come on."

"I don't look very good today."

"You always look great. You're the most photogenic person I know."

"Okay." Amber sighed and sat down where he directed her. That's why he loved her—she was always willing to help out, anyone and everyone.

He placed Mistletoe carefully above them and Amber secured the tiny dog in place with a harness so she wouldn't fall. Thankfully, she was docile and willing to stay in any position they placed her in.

"Now what?" Amber asked, watching Mistletoe carefully.

He sat facing Amber, their heads immediately below the Yorkie. "Now we get Mistletoe to look down at us, like she's encouraging us to kiss. I'll take a lot of shots, and we should get some that'll work. Here—use this to get her to look down at us."

Amber took the squeaky toy and squeezed it. The dog immediately cocked her head and stared down at them.

"No, too soon," Dillon said. "I wasn't ready. Plus, we need to look like we're kissing."

"Too bad. It would have been a good one."

"Yeah. Come on now, move closer."

Keeping their eyes on the Yorkie above, they moved closer to each other, so close he could feel Amber's breath on his face. "Now pucker up."

She thrust out her lips in a parody of a kiss. He couldn't help it, he laughed. That didn't keep him from taking pictures, though, since the dog was watching them curiously.

"Make it look natural, Amber, like you want to be kissed, not like you're trying to put your lips out as far as you can to keep me away. Maybe look a little dreamy."

She shot him a glare, then composed her face. "How's this?"

He stilled for a moment as she stared at him like he was her perfect match, her eyes soft, her lips slightly parted. Wow

—the guy who ended up on the receiving end of that look would be one lucky dude.

"Perfect," he declared and leaned in, clicking the remote to take as many pictures as possible.

They were so busy trying to keep their expressions moony at the same time as they watched Mistletoe that their lips met accidentally. Surprised, Dillon didn't even think to pull away. She had the softest lips....

He leaned in closer, hoping she'd attribute it to the necessity of getting the shot just right.

A voice suddenly came from the doorway. "You want I should go get Match?"

They jerked away from each other, and Dillon stifled a groan. It was Janice Carter, one of the town's biggest gossips, and her eyes gleamed with interest.

Amber scrambled to her feet, grabbing Mistletoe before she could fall. "No, no, of course not. We were just pretending to kiss—for the pictures for the website." She held up the dog. "You see, this is Mistletoe, so we were pretending to kiss below her like people do when they get below real mistletoe, though sometimes it's not really real..." She shook her head, her face flaming red. "Well, you get the idea."

Dillon held back a chuckle as he got to his feet. He rarely saw Amber babble.

"Uh huh," Janice said doubtfully. "Well, I just wanted to talk to you about getting volunteers for a Christmas party to benefit Sanctuary."

Amber still looked flustered—which would no doubt add fuel to the gossip fire. "Sounds like a good idea, but you should talk to Kat Channing—she's the new volunteer coordinator."

"Where can I find her?"

"In the office next to Mom's," Amber said hurriedly, almost shooing Janice in that direction.

"Okay," the gossip said, and left, but not without shooting a speculative glance back at them. A small smile played about her mouth. "I always did think you two should be together," she declared just before she closed the door.

Amber gave a half moan, half scream. "Argh! Well, now our 'kiss' will be all over Dogwood in what, an hour?"

"More like five minutes," Dillon said as he checked some of the photos on the camera. "Sorry about that."

She shrugged. "Not your fault. Besides, now people won't be surprised if they see us 'dating.'" This time, she used the air quotes. She slanted him a glance. "Did you plan that?" she asked in an accusing tone.

"Of course not," he assured her.

But he might have to plan for it to happen again—and not as an accident next time.

❦ ❦ ❦ ❦

TWO WEEKS LATER, Amber climbed into Dillon's car with Mistletoe. It seemed strange to be going on a "date" with Dillon. Strange, but good. At least she didn't have to worry about impressing him. He knew everything there was to know about her. Which would have been scary, if this was a real date.

"So, Mistletoe has become quite the star, hasn't she?" Dillon asked.

Amber rolled her eyes. "Yeah." Wouldn't you know it, the only picture of Mistletoe that hadn't made the dog look derpy was the one where they were kissing—with Amber all lovey-dovey and dopey-looking.

That kiss... Who knew that kissing your best friend would feel like such a revelation? No wonder he was so popular with the ladies. If one accidental kiss made *her* heart go pitty-pat, no telling what it did to other women.

Not that she'd *ever* tell Dillon that.

Once that picture had hit the internet—coupled with Janice's gossip—they'd received no end of nudges and sly winks. And now *everyone* wanted Mistletoe at their holiday events, in hope she'd turn out to be some kind of Match. Amber wanted to set them straight, but she couldn't without everyone realizing Dillon was just her pity date at the wedding.

She sighed. She'd have to put up with it until after New Year's, which was when they'd decided to stage their break-up.

Right now, Senior Village had requested Mistletoe for their holiday party, and since Dillon had already agreed to provide a photo booth with props for the residents to take pictures, they naturally assumed Amber would come with him.

As Dillon headed toward Senior Village, he said, "I'm surprised Mistletoe hasn't been adopted yet."

"Are you kidding? Everyone wants to adopt Mistletoe—or have her appear at their holiday parties. We had to take her off the site right away." Along with that embarrassing picture, thank goodness.

"So her new owner let her do these appearances?"

Amber squirmed a little. "Yeah, sure."

Dillon gave her a skeptical look. "Okay, I know that guilty look. Tell me the truth."

"What do you mean?" Amber hedged.

"Did you steal her from her new mom and dad?"

"Of course not!" Amber shoved his arm. "I adopted her."

"You?" Dillon hooted. "You said you'd never adopt another dog from Sanctuary—that it was unfair to the dogs you take care of there."

"I know, but...she's so adorable. Look at this sweet little face." The pup really did look incredibly cute in her red Christmas cape. They were at a stop sign, so she held Mistletoe up to Dillon's face. Mistletoe, who had adapted very quickly to life as a pampered pet, gave Dillon a kiss on the nose.

Dillon wrinkled his nose. "Slimy. But cute."

Yeah, right. As if he minded. He rubbed the dog's ears before merging back into traffic.

Amber laughed. "Besides, too many people wanted to adopt her for the wrong reasons."

"And you didn't?" Dillon asked with a raised eyebrow.

She didn't dignify that with a response.

He knew her well enough to take that as a denial. "Come on, tell me you're not thinking of using Mistletoe as your own personal Match, just like everyone else."

No, but Mistletoe did remind her of that strangely magical moment when they'd accidentally kissed. "Consider yourself told," she said firmly. "That would imply we are soul mates, and you know that's not true." *Too bad.*

Whoa. Where did that thought come from?

"Oh, yeah," he said thoughtfully. "I didn't think about that."

Wait a minute—he sounded wistful. Was he hoping this was real?

Naw—couldn't be. Could it?

❀ ❀ ❀ ❀

DILLON FOUND the party at Senior Village quite entertaining. The residents of the senior independent living facility were in the mood to have fun, and really enjoyed the photo booth, even using all the props.

Amber had steadfastly refused to let them perch

Mistletoe above their heads, explaining it was too dangerous for the tiny dog.

But one vivacious single woman named Helen insisted on having Mistletoe in her picture. "Come on," she insisted to Amber. "My grandson can hold her above our heads. He's very trustworthy, and Mistletoe will be perfectly safe."

Amber looked harassed, but Helen called out, "Liam, come here, dear."

Liam, a good-looking man about Dillon's age, came forward. "Yes, Nana?"

"Would you be a dear and hold Mistletoe above our heads for a picture? We need to keep her safe."

"Her?" he asked, giving Amber a puzzled look.

"The Yorkie, dear. Her name is Mistletoe. Her owner's name is Amber."

He glanced at the dog, but his gaze strayed more toward Amber than Mistletoe. "Sure," Liam said enthusiastically.

Dillon resisted the urge to roll his eyes. Amber looked especially pretty today. He wondered if the guy would be quite so enthusiastic if Mistletoe had been owned by one of his grandmother's friends.

"I don't know," Amber said reluctantly, but her eyes said something entirely different. Liam was just her type—tall, dark, and good-looking. A cliché walking. Dillon knew that look—she was sizing him up as a potential soul mate. "Will Mistletoe be safe?" she asked.

"An itty bitty dog like that?" Liam said with a grin. "I think I can hold onto her with no problem."

"Okay," Amber said, making Dillon grind his teeth.

"That won't work," Dillon objected. "He'll be in the picture."

But Helen wouldn't be deterred. "No problem. We'll get one of those tablecloths and hold it in front of him—they left some extras in the room."

Dillon considered the red tablecloths. The color was good, but... "I'm not sure that'll work."

"Why not?" Amber asked. "I can hold it up in front of Liam while he holds Mistletoe above their heads." She gave him her patented innocent look, which meant she was feeling anything but.

Irritated, but not understanding why he felt so annoyed, Dillon couldn't think of a good reason to refuse. "Okay," he said reluctantly.

Liam placed a chair in the back of the area they'd designated as a photo booth, then stood on it. Amber handed him the dog. True to his word, Liam was able to hold the Yorkie's rear in one big hand while posing her front legs with the other.

"We'll need a couple of people to hold the cloth," Dillon said.

"No problem," Amber said. "I can do it by myself—like this." She turned to face Liam, then held the tablecloth in her upraised hands behind her.

Oh, great. Now Amber was standing face to belly button with the hot guy. But since Dillon couldn't find a good reason to insist she turn around, he had to keep his mouth shut. Best to get this over with quickly. "Okay, Helen. Let's go."

Glee lit her eyes, and she said, "Just a minute."

Darting into the crowd, she grabbed one gentleman by the arm. He'd been surrounded by women all night, and Dillon had learned he was one of the few single men in the complex.

"C'mon, Lloyd," she said. "Let's take a picture."

Lloyd looked a little startled, but came along willingly.

"Okay," he said, and glanced at the props. "Shall I wear a Santa hat?"

"No, that won't be necessary," Helen said, and positioned

him just where she wanted him. She shot Dillon a warning glance. "Now, make sure to get this."

Dillon nodded and held the camera to his eye. He could hear Amber giggling behind the tablecloth and wondered what the heck was going on there. He focused above the cloth and saw Liam grinning. What a jerk.

"Look," Helen told Lloyd, pointing at the dog. "Mistletoe. You know what that means, don't you?"

Through Dillon's lens, Lloyd looked gobsmacked. "Mistletoe?" he repeated in befuddlement.

"Yes, so you have to kiss me."

Lloyd looked dismayed, but that didn't deter Helen. She grabbed his face with both hands and planted a big smooch on him. Dillon took the photo, but he wasn't sure either of them would want a copy. "Got it," he said. "We're done," he called to Amber as Lloyd backed away, his eyes wide.

"Us next!" a woman said. "C'mon, Jim. Let's kiss beneath Mistletoe."

There were a whole chorus of "Me, too"s and Dillon repressed a groan. Amber, who had lowered the tablecloth reluctantly, grinned.

"Hey, Lloyd," Dillon called out. "Can you hold one end of that tablecloth for Amber so she won't get tired?" That way he'd get Amber a little farther away from Liam and save poor Lloyd from any more ambush kisses. Two birds, one stone.

"Sure," Lloyd said enthusiastically, shooting him a grateful look.

After he had taken a picture of practically every couple under Mistletoe, some wanted to come back for more, but Dillon had to call a halt. "That's enough. I'm sure Mistletoe is tired, and probably needs to take a break. Wouldn't want her emulating our town fountain on your heads."

Everyone laughed, and Liam got down from the chair and

handed Mistletoe to Amber with a grin and a sparkle in his eyes.

"Here, I'll help," Dillon said, and took Mistletoe from Amber. He turned toward the door, but Amber didn't move. Instead, she smiled up at Liam.

Putting his hand at the small of Amber's back, Dillon added, "I need to talk to you...alone."

Once they were outside in the cold air, and Mistletoe was searching for a suitable place to water the lawn, Amber said, "So, what did you want to talk about?"

Dillon grimaced. "Did you want us to 'break up' before the wedding?"

"What?" she asked in surprise. "Why?"

"The way you were flirting with Liam..."

She gaped at him. "Are you *jealous*?"

"No, of course not." Though a little voice deep inside called him a liar. "But no one will believe we're together if you're giggling with someone else."

"Oh," she said, and realization seemed to dawn on her. "I forgot about that."

"I figured. Flirting with every attractive guy is just something you do."

"What does that mean?" she asked indignantly.

"Just telling it like it is. You're so bent on finding your soul mate that you look for him in every single guy you see." He shrugged. "I didn't say there was anything wrong with it —it's just something you do."

She sighed. "Yeah, I guess it's a habit."

"But not one you should indulge when you're supposed to have a boyfriend."

She glared at him. "You have a point. How can we fix this?"

Dillon didn't even have to think about it. "Easy. You can act, right?" At her nod, he said, "Then just follow my lead."

Amber followed him back into the party, and when Liam came forward, Dillon handed him the dog. "Just one more picture," he said with a smile.

Liam looked taken aback, but good-naturedly took his place on the chair with the Yorkie. "And, Lloyd, can you hold the cloth?"

"Sure," the man said.

As Lloyd held the cloth, Dillon grabbed Amber's hand and positioned her beneath Mistletoe, making sure Liam had a good view of them. The camera was already on the tripod, so all he needed was his remote. "Our turn," he told Amber.

Her eyes opened wide, but before she could say anything, he leaned in for the kiss and captured her lips with his. He held her close and used all his acting abilities to make it look like he was a man in love and that she was the only woman in the world.

It worked so well, he even convinced himself. Their lips met and clung, then met again, deeper, firmer. He wanted to drown in her, take her all in, and never let her go.

When the cat calls and hooting registered in his fogged brain, he pulled away, and Amber looked as shell-shocked as he did.

He glanced down at the remote in his hand. "I, uh, forgot to take the picture."

"No problem," Jim said from behind his camera. "I saw that you were a bit preoccupied, so I took it for you. Got a lot of them, actually."

"Uh, thanks," Dillon said, though he wouldn't have minded a reason to kiss her again.

Amber glanced up as Liam handed her the dog, and her face was flushed. Liam's face, on the other hand, was closed and stern.

Mission accomplished.

OVER THE NEXT WEEK, Amber spent a lot of time thinking about Dillon. Far more than she'd ever thought about her best friend before, and in a totally different way.

Holy cow, that kiss...

She'd always wanted someone to kiss her that way, like she was his entire universe. And the fact that it was her best friend, playing a part, who made her feel so special was...confusing. Especially when he posted the pictures of the party on their website and she saw how very convincing he was. Okay, to be honest, they both were. But on her part, the reaction had been genuine.

Amber had problems remembering that it was just pretend, and was afraid that would show in her face, so she'd reined in her natural tendency to flirt with Dillon, except when they were in public.

She wanted to explore that kiss again...and again, and again, to tell the truth, but it was out of the question. Dillon was only play-acting, to help her out at the wedding, and after New Year's, they'd go back to being just best friends. If they could.

They had to. Even if she and Dillon weren't *together* together, she couldn't lose him as a friend—she just couldn't. Who else would she share her day with, who else would laugh with her at the silly antics of the dogs and townspeople, who else would be able to share her thoughts with a single glance?

She sighed. If the only way to keep Dillon in her life was to play this strange farce out, then go back to the way they'd always been, that's what she'd do.

But first, the wedding. She glanced in the mirror, and had to admit she was looking her best in a coral dress with a sweetheart neckline. It hugged her curves, then flared out just above her knees. She didn't try to analyze why she wanted to look her absolute best for this—she just did.

When Dillon picked her up, his reaction was all she could have asked for...from a real date, anyway. His eyes widened as he looked her up and down. "You look... You look..."

"Acceptable?" she asked, whirling in a circle.

"More than that," he declared enthusiastically. "You look stunning. I have to shoot you in that!"

She laughed. Not because he thought she looked stunning, of course, but because the photography comment was pure Dillon.

"Oh, good. Then let's go."

She let him help her on with her coat and they headed toward the McPherson ranch for the wedding. The barn, to be specific. It was one place that would hold the huge clan, and Bliss and Luke had a lot of family hereabouts. Luckily, Helen, who'd had no luck with Lloyd, had declared that Mistletoe was no Match, so the poor dog could be left at home in her cozy bed.

Dillon helped her out of the car, and led her to the barn. She gasped as she entered. It was gorgeous, decorated in white tulle with yellow roses, daisies, and lots of twinkling fairy lights. Very rustic chic.

The wedding was just as lovely. Bliss was a vision in white lace, Luke looked darkly handsome, and even Bliss's border collie, the newest Match, was adorable as the proud ring bearer. The two of them seemed made for each other, and Amber sternly suppressed her envy. *I want that.*

Afterward, as she and Dillon danced to a slow song by the country-western band at the reception, Amber sighed. This was just too perfect. She was glad he'd volunteered to be her date, but now she never wanted it to end. And end it would, in a week or so.

"What's wrong?" Dillon asked. "You've been acting strange the past few weeks."

"Yeah—acting. I guess I'm just tired of acting. I just want it to be over with."

"You do?" Dillon asked, looking hurt. He drew her aside, behind some hay bales. In the privacy of their sheltered area, he peered down at her. "I kind of thought you were...enjoying this."

"Oh, I am," she admitted. "But everyone assumes we're going to be together forever."

"Would that be so terrible?" he asked softly.

She glanced up in surprise. "I just hate deceiving everyone."

"Well, it's not deceit if it's really true."

Her heart leapt like a wild thing in her chest. "What do you mean?" she asked, feeling suddenly breathless.

"To tell you the truth, Amber, I can't stop thinking about you...as more than just a friend, I mean."

"Me, too," she said softly. "But it's just the playacting, right? It's not real. Right?" she asked, hoping to be contradicted.

He shook his head. "It's no longer acting on my part. I have feelings for you—feelings I never expected. I've always loved you, but no I'm falling *in* love with you. I kind of want to know how it will play out."

Amber's heart leapt again at the look in his eyes. "You do?"

"Indubitably," he said with a grin, then sobered. "What about you?"

"I feel the same way. That's why I've been acting funny around you. I'm not sure whether to treat you as a boy friend, or a *boyfriend*."

He chuckled. "I'm the same person either way. Just treat me however you feel."

Definitely as a boyfriend. "But...what if we break up for real some day? We can't lose our friendship." That would be devastating.

"We'll make a pact here and now. We try this out, and if it doesn't work, we'll still remain friends, no matter what. Okay?"

She definitely wanted to try it. Falling in love with her best friend—and she had to admit that's what she'd done—was the best of both worlds. Was it worth the risk, to try a deeper relationship, but potentially lose his friendship, no matter what pact they made?

She gazed up into his eyes, and saw all his feelings reflected there. *Yes, it is.* If she could only see that every day for the rest of her life, her life would be complete.

"Okay," she said.

I just hope this isn't a terrible mistake. But she was sure going to enjoy the heck out of finding out.

He hugged her and leaned in for a kiss, but Janice rounded the corner. "Come on, you two love birds," she said. "It's time to throw the bouquet."

As all the single women gathered around, Bliss tossed the bouquet. It seemed to hang in mid-air for a moment, then dropped straight into Amber's arms.

She glanced down at it in surprise, and Dillon was suddenly there. "Think it's a sign?" he asked.

She shrugged. "Maybe." But there was only one sign she trusted. And Match had never put them together, though the dog had had plenty of chances. All her life, in fact.

"Okay," Luke shouted. "Now the single guys. Line up, and I'll throw the garter."

"That's your cue," Amber whispered, and Dillon went into the line-up.

Luke made a big production out of removing the blue

garter from Bliss's shapely thigh, then turned his back on the men. "Here it comes."

He tossed the garter and it flew through the air, but never reached the outstretched hands. Instead, Match leapt up and snatched it out of the air. Everyone gasped and laughed, murmuring in surprise. What did Match want with it?

Looking proud as punch, Match made a beeline for Dillon, and placed one end in his waiting hand.

Amber gasped. Was this it? Was this the sign she'd waited for all her life?

Her heart in her throat, she watched Dillon grasp one side of the garter as Match held onto the other. They both glanced at her.

"Get over there, girl," someone said.

Her heart soaring, she made her way to Dillon's side. "Are you trying to tell us something, Match?" she asked breathlessly.

Match made one sharp yip and glanced up at the ceiling where a bough of mistletoe hung directly above them.

"That's a yes," Dillon said. "I guess Match just had to wait until we were ready."

"You're ready?"

"Yes. I love you, Amber."

"Ditto," Amber said and melted into his arms as everyone cheered.

Finally, Match found my soul mate. And it was definitely worth the wait.

THE SUGAR COOKIE MIRACLE

BY JODI ANDERSON

LANA HENDERSON GAVE one last kick, hitting the most delicate of parts on the monstrosity. Right in the coils. A whir and a gurgle followed.

Turn back on, darn you.

Losing a refrigerator and freezer full of food was not an option. Not on her nonexistent budget with Christmas only two weeks away.

The strains of a holiday song about family and everyone coming home for Christmas drifted from the radio in the living room, filled with hope, promises, and yearning. Lana squeezed her eyes closed against the sadness that threatened to produce tears.

I will not cry. Not anymore.

It had been a long road. Literally and figuratively. A road filled with more than enough angst and tears. No way was she bringing that heartache forward into their new life.

Dogwood was a fresh start. The place Lana could finally create safety and roots for herself and Sam. This was their home now. And though they might be family poor, they had each other.

That is enough. She would make it enough.

A home was way overdue for her nine-year-old son. And for Lana. Thirty-two, and she'd yet to have a yard of her own to plant even a measly flower, much less the vegetable garden she'd always secretly yearned for.

The gurgle of the old fridge was followed by the soft hum of the motor resurrecting.

Yes!

Score another one for the woman who learned her "handyman" skills on the internet as she stumbled along. Lana had answered the ad for an onsite handyman that offered a small cottage—rent-free—in exchange for helping her new landlady, Emma Pickler, maintain her little rental cottages and property.

Glancing at the clock, Lana realized it was more than time to start dinner since Sam should be getting home from his scout meeting anytime. A mom Lana had met last week offered to carpool and drop Sam off since they drove right past on their way home from the meeting.

Wonder if Sam and Emma would like tacos?

Lana always offered dinner to Emma if she saw her car was in the drive. Although independent, the lady was well into her eighties, and Lana worried about her.

Putting the toolbox back in the bottom of the miniscule pantry closet, Lana scrubbed the grime off her hands before preparing dinner. It might not be fancy fare, but it would be good.

Cooking was something that she'd taken pride in the past decade during her now-ended marriage. With the amount of time Steve had been on the road with his band, Lana had thrown herself into being a mom, as well as mastering the art of stretching a buck. That included their food budget. So, although the meals might be plain, Lana tried to put a little extra time and love into them to make them delicious and special.

A horn sounded outside, and she slid the pan of browning meat to a cool burner.

My boy is home. Joy pulsed through her as it always did when thinking of Sam. She loved nothing more than spending time with him.

Grabbing her coat off the coat rack as she passed, Lana stepped out into the frigid night. A late-model SUV was parked near the bottom step of the small porch with its window rolled down on her side.

"Hey, Cindy" Lana smiled at the woman she'd met at the first scout meeting. "Thank you so much for bringing Sam home. Had to get the refrigerator working."

The woman inside waved a hand in the air. "It was my turn, and Sam is never any bother. He helps Blaine keep Gage happy on the drive."

The toddler in the car seat between the two boys in the backseat giggled as Sam and Blaine took turns tickling under his chin.

How did my son learn to be so kind?

But Lana knew how. Sam had been born gentle— he knew no other way. Even without the influence of a father most of the time, somehow, her boy had learned how to treat other people well.

"My turn next week, then." Lana opened the back door and Sam gave one final tickle before he slid down to the ground.

As soon as they'd waved his friends off, Sam grabbed her around the waist. "It was the best, Mom. Our troop leader told us all about a campout next summer that is for two whole nights away. Can I go, can I?"

Lana's heart clenched at the thought. First, at the thought of Sam being away for multiple overnights. Second, at the possible expense. She'd have to chat with Claire and see if she had any info so that Lana would be able to find a way to make it happen if it meant being around some positive male role models.

"That sounds great, bud." Lana returned his squeeze. Luckily, Sam was still at the age where hugging Mom didn't appear to be a faux paus yet.

Thank heavens.

Chatting non-stop about his spelling test at school, stories about elementary school drama, and the outdoor skills they'd learned at their meeting, Sam walked next to Lana into their cozy cottage.

"Goodness, did that really happen at recess?" Lana laughed as Sam wrapped up his story. "How about you put your backpack in your room and wash up for dinner? Taco night."

Giving an excited punch in the air above his head, Sam traveled down the short hallway off the living room to his bedroom at the back of the small house. Lana could hear his excited chant of "Tacos. Tacos." as he did as she'd asked. Good thing her son was easy to please, and would eat just about anything she prepared. But tacos were his absolute favorite.

Setting plates at their small table under the window in the farthest corner of the living area, Lana dialed Emma's number.

"Hi, Emma." She patiently waited while Emma went through her normal questions about Lana and Sam's day. Lana answered each of them, then quickly slipped in her usual evening ploy where she pretended to have made too much dinner again and offered to have Emma over or take her a plate.

"You are such a dear, Lana." Emma gave a small laugh. "But, you know I'm on to you. How I ever got so lucky to have you move in with your handyman skills and generous cooking skills, I'll never know."

Lana silently begged forgiveness for her small exaggeration about her fix-it skills to get this home for herself and Sam. Luckily, there wasn't anything she hadn't been able to find on the internet to help her keep up with the small repair requests, so far.

"We are the lucky ones, Emma. And I just want to make sure you are eating well," Lana admitted.

"How about we agree that we are both lucky?" Emma said. "But, I'm set for dinner tonight. My friend Myrtle...you know Myrtle down at the Crack-of-Dawn Donut shop?"

"Sam and I met her when we picked up donuts for his birthday celebration at school a couple of weeks ago." Lana remembered balking at the cost, but it was the only thing her son had asked for on his birthday. The miniscule tabletop ping pong set that hooked up to their table had been a lucky bonus find at the resale shop in Pueblo before they'd moved. She'd squirreled it away until Sam's birthday, and he'd enjoyed it almost as much as the donuts. "Myrtle was so kind to Sam and made him feel extra special."

"That's Myrtle, all right. Well, she's picking me up, and we're meeting a couple of other ladies at The Spot for dinner," Emma shared. "It's their meatloaf supreme special tonight."

"Sounds lovely," Lana said as she waved Sam to the table when he came back into the room. "You ladies be safe."

After a quick goodbye, Lana sat in the chair opposite her son. "Well, Emma is going out on the town with friends, so I hope you don't mind leftover tacos for dinner tomorrow night?"

"That's awesome!" Sam smiled. "Thanks, Mom."

As they ate dinner and laughed about what Sam imagined

a Taco Dragon might look like, Lana filed every minute into the special memories file in her brain.

This. This is what makes it all worthwhile.

This week, Lana would officially reopen the little bridal shop and event planning business she'd managed to takeover that prompted their relocation to Dogwood. Between the duties taking care of Emma's cottages and her new business, Lana would be busy.

But, for Sam, she'd do whatever it took to secure their future and create the home they both wanted...no, needed.

Finally.

❦ ❦ ❦ ❦

CHRIS GREEN CHECKED his directions again. Yup, he was finally on the last stretch of highway that would take him into Dogwood, Colorado. In the middle of nowhere. At least that's what it felt like after spending most of his time in New York the past three years.

Although he'd known Luke since they'd met in college on the east coast, Chris had never visited Luke's hometown. But, being asked to be his friend's best man seemed as good a time as any.

Where is that turnoff?

Finally, on the right, he saw the faint sign that indicated the road north of town that would take him to Luke's family ranch. A few feet beyond the turn was a faded wooden sign that read, EMMA'S COTTAGES. RENTALS BY THE WEEK OR MONTH. Although faded, the words were faintly visible in the glare of his brights. He could make out a small cottage in the trees.

This really isn't New York.

Chris watched for the landmark Luke mentioned and turned into the drive that would take him to his destination.

Hopefully, a warm bed for himself and wedded bliss for his best friend waited in Dogwood.

He chuckled to himself. Wedded bliss. Since Luke's fiancé's name was Bliss, it seemed a good omen. But though marriage might be bliss for his friend, it definitely wasn't for Chris. He had plans, goals, and a company to grow and expand. Marriage and settling down were not in the picture.

At least, not for a *very* long time.

LANA TUCKED Sam in following dinner clean-up, homework, and a quick shower. Smiling, Sam snuggled in with his favorite teddy bears—Dexter and Rocky.

Closing his door until it was only open a crack, Lana headed back to her paperwork and computer for the final run-through on the numbers for the business. If all went well, she'd take over the two weddings currently being planned by the lady retiring who'd kindly spent two weeks showing Lana the ropes.

Rolling her neck and allowing her eyes to close for a moment, Lana smiled. This was what she enjoyed. Helping others create events to remember. Although she hadn't had the traditional white wedding since she'd eloped with Steve, Lana had dreamed of what it was like. An online program had taught her skills she needed to supplement her built-in passion for creating magical events.

The two weddings she'd inherited could make or break her in a small town. Especially the first one, only two weeks away. On Christmas Eve. The groom, a town favorite son, and the bride, recently returned to her hometown and an attorney. Both came from founding families of Dogwood.

No pressure, Lana. No pressure at all.

❦ ❦ ❦ ❦

CATCHING up with Luke had only taken minutes since they communicated via email and phone daily with the business. Once they'd made the motions and he'd stashed his suitcase in the small guest house, Chris settled in front of the fire at the main house. Luke sat in the matching recliner.

"So, when do I get to meet the woman who finally roped and branded you?" Chris asked.

Luke chuckled. "Just wait. Make fun of it all you want, but when it happens to you, I'll remind you of all your negative talk about relationships and marriage."

Chris shook his head, but kept silent. He'd seen enough train-wreck relationships to know it would be a long time, if ever, before he took that kind of step.

"We meet Bliss at the bridal shop first thing in the morning." Luke crouched in front of the fire and used the poker to expose the heart of the fire before adding a last log.

Bridal shop.

The words made Chris want to beg off, but he'd support his friend in whatever way Luke and his bride asked.

The next morning, after breakfast with Milt, they headed to town and grabbed coffee at a place called Belly-Up before meeting Bliss in front of the Great Expectations Event Planning storefront.

"Finally, the man, the legend." Bliss stepped forward and, instead of shaking his hand, grabbed Chris in a hug. "So you are the guy I hear about all day long. Suppose I should be jealous of Luke's 'work wife', but in this case, I'm okay with it."

Taken aback for only a moment, Chris returned the hug of the gorgeous brunette. "And I'll try not to worry that you're dragging Luke into matrimony land."

Bliss laughed and stepped next to Luke. "Is that what he told you?"

"Fine, I'm the one who didn't want to wait till next summer and pushed for a Christmas wedding." Luke didn't look embarrassed. "Didn't want you getting away again."

When the couple kissed and nuzzled, Chris almost envied his friend who'd found who was obviously the right woman for him.

❦ ❦ ❦ ❦

THROUGH THE HAND-CROCHETED lace valance on the bottom of the front picture window, Lana watched a small group of people meet with hugs and laughter. The two men were both handsome with easy smiles and laughter.

I wonder which one is the groom?

Not that it mattered—she had an event to create, and no time or inclination to be looking at men. She took a deep breath and angled her chin upward a smidge.

You've got this, girl. This is your gift.

Making special events and occasions memorable and unique was the thing that fulfilled her. It was what she could offer the world. Second only to Sam. He was her contribution to the planet that made her the proudest—Lana's most important job.

Stepping to the door, Lana turned the deadbolt and opened the heavy half glass, half wooden door. A gust of chill wind swept inside, smelling of the forecasted snow to come.

The group on the sidewalk turned toward her.

"Good morning! I have warm drinks, fresh apricot scones, and sugar cookies ready for you." Lana moved back a step and let the three visitors pass inside.

"Lana!" Bliss greeted her immediately.

Finding herself wrapped in a warm hug, Lana laughed. "I'm happy to see you, too."

Although she'd only met Bliss twice while transitioning the wedding, it felt more than comfortable to be around her.

Bliss pulled Lana over to the men. She grabbed the denim coat sleeve on the closest one. "This is my fiancé, Luke McPherson."

That solves the question of which man is the lucky guy.

The tall, good-looking man caught Lana's hand in a firm handshake. "Pleased to finally meet you. Sounds like you are pulling out all the stops to give us a humdinger of a wedding."

Lana could feel heat in her cheeks. "I hope so—it's what I love doing."

Motioning to Lana, Bliss pointed to the other man who'd come in with them. "Chris, come meet Lana. Lana, this is Luke's best friend...and the best man. Chris Green. He came in from New York for the wedding."

The man turned toward her, and Lana was drawn to his easy smile.

Shaking his hand, Lana hoped he wouldn't feel the slight tremor in her fingers from meeting him. Hoped he would simply assume she was chilled. "Pleased to meet you, Chris. Welcome to Dogwood. Is this your first time here?"

Stop talking, Lana. You're prattling.

Chris turned and shook the hand of the woman Bliss introduced as the event planner. All he noticed were her beautiful, wide eyes and trembling fingers. She must have gotten cold holding the door for them.

"First time. Though I'm embarrassed to admit it. Luke's been trying to get me out here for years." Chris motioned out the front window where snowflakes were now falling. "Any place you recommend I check out while I'm here?"

Lana laughed softly. "I'm hardly an expert. Only been here for a couple of months myself."

Bliss joined them. "Sanctuary—definitely visit Sanctuary so you know what Dogwood is all about."

"You mean the animal rescue place?" Lana asked.

"It's that, and much more." Bliss smiled. "We'll make sure you guys get to see it before the wedding."

Lana motioned toward the table where a coffee carafe and plate of scones and cookies awaited. "Well, let's get this show on the road so we can finalize plans."

Chris moved with everyone else to grab a fresh cup of coffee and food.

An hour later, Chris rubbed the back of his neck. While everyone else seemed energized by all of the details, he needed to get some fresh air.

"So, you all seem to have things handled here. Mind if I skip out and meet up with you later?"

Luke waved him off. "Do your thing. We'll text you later about lunch."

Chris put on his coat and warm hat. The snow that had been sporadic before was now a light, steady fall.

"Lana, thank you for the coffee. I'm sure I'll see you later." He shook her hand, noting how small it felt in his.

The woman's only response was a nod and a blush. Or was the blush only his imagination?

❄ ❄ ❄ ❄

LANA FORCED herself to stay focused on the drawings and design boards on the conference table, but she was too aware of Chris, even his nods and shared conversations with Bliss and Luke. The man was a distraction.

And a distraction was the last thing she needed.

The next hour flew by with the bride and groom making

final choices on the last details of the wedding and reception. Both the ceremony and reception would be held at the barn on the McPherson ranch.

While not fancy, she'd heard it had a down-home ambiance and plenty of space. Having everything in one place certainly simplified things for Lana.

Now, if only I could keep my mind from wandering back to that distracting man.

It's not as if they'd spent a lot of time together, but his smile and easy demeanor had made him memorable and comfortable to be around. And since he was acting as an unofficial photographer for the wedding when he wasn't taking care of his best man duties, Lana would need to meet with him at least once more to coordinate some of the activities for that day.

Then, he'd leave and head back to New York. No sense getting to know someone who was only a temporary fixture in Dogwood.

Especially one who made Lana wish he weren't.

❄️❄️❄️❄️

CHRIS SPENT an hour or so walking and exploring Dogwood in the light snow. Though he'd followed Luke into town in his own car so he could come and go as he pleased, Chris wanted to see the town on foot.

Photography might be mostly a hobby right now, but he couldn't help seeing everything through that filter. The lighting. The symmetry. The everyday activities going on around town. Imagining how each angle might look through a camera lens.

Though he spent most of his time in major cities around the world, Chris understood the draw most folks must feel to Dogwood. It felt solid. Like it was in many ways the same as it had been for a hundred years or more, but also moving forward. With purpose.

It was clear to Chris what that purpose was after visiting a half dozen businesses and interacting with some of the residents. They had each been bound and determined to make him feel welcome. To learn about him. And to share about their pride and joy. Sanctuary. The whole town seemed animal-happy.

Huh. And I've never even had a hamster.

Being a military kid growing up, then traveling the world with the nonprofit he and Luke had started, hadn't left Chris a lot of time for a pet. Not the kind of time they needed and deserved.

Maybe someday.

Chris pulled his phone out to check the text that came through.

Are you available for lunch at The Spot?

Luke assumed Chris knew what The Spot was and, luckily, he'd seen it a block over while exploring the town. Since the chill had seeped into his bones, Chris thought a warm lunch sounded great. He texted back that he'd be there.

It's not New York City winter cold, but that bite in the North wind keeps it far from balmy. I hope this snow stops.

❧ ❧ ❧

LANA FINALIZED a few more notes in her computer for the Galore and McPherson wedding before rotating her neck and shutting the laptop. Although the appointment had ended more than two hours earlier, she'd been on the phone with vendors, updating them on changes and confirming times.

Lunchtime had come and gone. The coffee, scones, and cookies from the morning were a far-distant memory and her stomach was making its lack of contents known with loud grumbles.

Okay. Okay. I get it. I'll head home and eat.

After straightening her desk and the snack table, Lana locked the front door, turned off the lights, and headed toward the back door. Looking back into the dim interior of what was now *her* storefront, Lana smiled. She had a long way to go, but she'd already come a far piece.

It felt right.

Waiting for her old car to warm up, Lana checked her texts. Two from Emma with tenant requests. One for a relight on a pilot that had gone out on a water heater, and another for help changing a smoke detector battery. Neither sounded like something she couldn't handle.

Fingers crossed. Putting her car into gear, Lana headed out. She had two hours before Sam was due home. Time for researching, fixing, and, if lucky, a quick sandwich in there somewhere.

After changing into old jeans and a soft green sweatshirt, Lana wolfed down her thrown-together ham sandwich while watching an online tutorial on relighting a water heater. It looked straightforward, as long as she took precautions. And the battery change only required a ladder and a bit of nerve climbing to the top.

Luckily, many of Emma's cottage tenants were senior citizens, so odds were, they'd be home. With her tummy now quieted, a bit more knowledge in her head, a warm jacket, and her handy toolbox, Lana headed for the cantankerous water heater at Mr. Purlman's place.

The man responded almost immediately to her knock.

Must have been watching for me.

"Thanks, Lana. Sorry to bother you, but getting on the floor and trying to read how to restart that thing just isn't happening with my old knees." Mr. Perlman held the door open and ushered her inside. "Can't believe this snow. Thought it would have let up by now, but looks like it's coming down harder."

Lana smiled. He was a talker, and rarely noticed if it was mostly one-sided.

"How about some hot tea for your troubles when you're done?"

Much as she wanted to be done and on her way, Lana had quickly learned that the help she could provide to some of the older tenants was second to a listening and caring ear.

Shrugging out of her jacket, Lana nodded. "I can't stay too long, but I'd love a cup of tea. Let me see what I can do with your water heater."

Since the cottages all had the same floor plan, though sometimes reversed, she knew exactly where to go. After removing the small metal plate that covered the pilot light, Lana scanned the directions to confirm what she'd learned and went through the safety check and steps before pushing the relight button. After a couple of metallic clicks, it brought the tiny flame back to life.

Score one for the handywoman. Now for tea and conversation. Then on to the battery.

Mr. Purlman watched her replace the cover then wandered off to steep their tea. "Come on over to the table when you're ready."

Lana put her toolbox next to the front door, then washed her hands before taking a seat at the tiny wooden table. It had been the same routine the three other times she'd been here for minor fixes.

"So, are you going to Story Time at the library in the morning?" Lana asked as she nodded her thanks for the tea he placed in front of her.

"Since no one has asked me to run off and elope with them to Las Vegas this week, I suppose I'd better show up and not disappoint the little ones." He laughed at the retelling of his favorite joke.

"You know they love your stories. Especially the ones that include dragons and magic." She and Sam had stopped into one of the Story Times when they'd first moved to Dogwood, before school started. "We can't wait for the holiday break so Sam can come in again and listen."

Mr. Purlman nodded and smiled. "That Sam is a character. A good boy. You tell him to stop by sometime this evening so I can give him a little stocking I put together for him, if that's okay with you."

Lana's heart filled with more love for the town and these people. They'd been so accepting of her and Sam. "You are so good to us, Mr. Purlman. Of course Sam can have anything you want him to have."

After a few more minutes of small talk, Lana finished her tea and excused herself. It was getting close to the time Sam would be coming home on the bus, and there was still one more cottage to stop in to.

Changing the battery took only a few minutes once Lana realized the tenant was not home, but had left the key in its normal hiding place on the porch. With the short ladder and a nine-volt battery, the job was completed.

The handywoman scores again.

The squeal of the school bus's brakes heralded Sam's arrival home. Lana put away the files from the shop she'd worked on after the fixes were completed.

Sam ran into her arms where she waited in the open doorway. The covered porch kept most of the snowflakes from swirling inside with her bundle-of-energy son.

"It's snowing, Mom!"

Lana brushed the light layer of snow from her son's hat. "So it is. You know what that means, right?"

"Sugar cookies?" Sam walked inside the house.

"Of course. It's our tradition." Lana helped him tug his snow boots off. "And you can take some to Mr. Purlman, too. He says he has something for you."

If this snow slows down enough for Sam to get out once the cookies are done. Lana glanced out the window before refocusing on Sam.

"What is it? Did he tell you? Did you see it?" Sam's questions tumbled over each other in his excitement to get more information.

"Slow down, before you tie your tongue in a knot." Lana laughed and hugged him again. "Then, how would you eat any cookies? Let's get a batch in the oven before you get homework started."

"Woohoo!" Sam scrambled to put away his things before coming back to the kitchen. "Can I read the recipe this time?"

"Wouldn't have it any other way, buckaroo." Ever since Sam had learned to read, it had been important to him to help read recipes when they cooked together. And since it had encouraged him to learn some math, as well, with the measuring and adjusting when they doubled or halved dishes, it was a win-win.

"Can I take some to Miss Emma, too?" Sam asked.

"You know you can. She loves your cookies."

An hour and a half later, homework was done. Leftovers were reheated and eaten for dinner. And the cookies were portioned out carefully in plastic bowls with lids for Mr. Purlman and Miss Emma. Sam even placed a holiday-themed sticker on the center of each lid.

"Can I go by myself, Mom? I'm old enough."

Lana hesitated only a moment after peeking out the blinds and checking that the porch lights shone through the falling snow from both cottages. "Sure. But straight there and straight back, got it?"

Sam nodded eagerly through the layers of winter gear he'd piled on for the short journey.

Lana balanced the two bowls in his outstretched arms and held the door for him. After seeing Mr. Purlman open his door and usher Sam inside, Lana closed the door and hurried to clean up their dishes and baking mess before he came back.

Although exhausted, Lana still felt blessed beyond measure.

Life is good.

❄️ ❄️ ❄️ ❄️

CHRIS SQUINTED, trying to see through the snow hitting the windshield. He probably shouldn't have stayed in town so long, but he and Luke had run into a bunch of people Luke had known since high school.

Their dinner invite and poker game afterward had run longer than anyone had anticipated. Luke had gone on ahead since they had their own cars, and Chris needed a couple of items from the corner mart.

Where is the turn-off?

Surely he'd gone far enough. Coming from the direction of town and the snow falling made everything look way different than it had last night when he'd arrived.

Almost missing the turn, Chris slammed his brakes, and slid several feet. There was the faded sign for the rental cottages.

Take it easy, Chris. Don't want to end up in a ditch.

Slowing down to increase his visibility in the ever-heavier snow, Chris could barely make out the lights from the cottages on the right as he came alongside.

Out of the corner of his eye, he spotted a shape in the

ditch next to the road. *Surely that isn't a kid. Next to the road in heavy snow.*

Carefully tapping his brakes this time, Chris slowed until he stopped.

He rolled his window down. "Hey, you all right there?"

The small shape looked down toward his feet and appeared to try to bend and lift something.

Chris put the truck into park and shut off the engine. He didn't want to get out in the cold and snow, but he couldn't just drive off without making sure the kid was okay.

Walking closer, he pulled his collar higher against the flakes finding their way into his neckline. "Can I help with anything?"

The boy—he could see it was a boy now that he was closer—shook his head no. But, again, he knelt in the snow and tried to move a mound of white.

Chris moved closer, but slowly so he didn't startle the boy.

What in the world kind of game is the kid playing in this kind of weather?

Then the mound moved and whined. It was an animal, a dog.

The boy looked up at Chris. "I think he's hurt or something, but I can't lift him."

Chris knelt next to the boy. The dog appeared to be light-colored and medium-sized. "Want me to help get him in my truck so I can take you home?"

The boy peered at him, snowflakes still falling between them. "I don't know you."

"Good point. I'm Chris. How far is your house?"

The boy pointed toward the faint glow of light coming from the small grouping of cottages just visible in the truck's headlights.

"Okay, so, how about I turn off my truck and help you get your dog home? By the way, what's your name?"

The boy looked at Chris, down at the dog again, and then toward the cottages. He appeared to be weighing a decision. A whimper from the dog seemed to help him decide.

"I'm Sam. Hope Mom won't be mad."

Chris loped to move his truck farther off the road then ran back. The snowfall was heavier than ever. "So, I'm going to try to lift your dog. What's his name?"

Sam shook his head, "I don't know. He's not mine. I just heard him yelp, so I tried to help."

A stray, possibly. *Hope he's friendly.* Chris really didn't want a dog bite on top of the frostbite he was going to have if he didn't get out of the weather soon.

Sam crouched in the quickly accumulating snow, letting the dog sniff and lick his fingers.

"I gave him my sugar cookie."

"Good thinking. Looks like he liked it." Chris lowered himself next to the two. Cold and wet seeped into the fabric of his jeans.

He aimed the flashlight on his phone toward the dog.

Surprise.

"So, seems our 'he' is a 'she'...and a very pregnant one at that."

"Huh?" Sam looked up at Chris.

Even in the driving snow, Chris could see the look of confusion on his face.

I'm not getting into the birds and bees.

"Just that I think it's a girl dog and she may have babies on the way." Chris let the dog sniff his hand.

Carefully placing his hands under the dog to best support her, Chris slowly lifted her while talking softly to the dog. She couldn't weigh much more than thirty pounds or so.

Sam offered words of encouragement, too, and kept a hand on her head.

They headed through what was now a near white-out toward the glow of the cottages.

❄ ❄ ❄ ❄

LANA PEERED out the window again. Sam was gone a bit longer than she'd anticipated, but she was sure he was simply being polite and keeping either Emma or Mr. Purlman company for a bit.

I'll give him a couple of more minutes, then I'm going to go get him and bring him home. She didn't like how thick the snow was getting.

Just as the lights flickered and went out, a thump sounded on the front porch. Lana nearly tripped over a chair in her haste to let Sam in.

Sam's probably cold and scared, in the dark since the lights went out.

Lana yanked the door open, then gasped as Sam pushed inside with a large man carrying a child right behind him. No, not a child—a dog. The glow of the miniscule fireplace only barely lit the room. Details were difficult to make out.

"What in the world...Sam? Are you okay?" Lana pushed the door closed against the wind and blowing snow. She turned back to look at the man who was turned away from her and kneeling to place the dog on the rug in front of the fire. "Sir, what's going on?"

Lana pulled Sam closer and brushed the snow from his hood and shoulders.

"It's okay, Mom. This man helped me." Sam pointed toward the two in front of the fire.

The man in question patted the dog again, then turned.

Lana gasped. "Chris?" It was the man she'd met that morning. The best man from Bliss's wedding.

He stood. "Small world, Lana. This must be your son then. He's quite a responsible young man. Sam heard an animal in need and wouldn't leave her in this snowstorm. I happened to see them in the ditch when I turned the corner."

Lana looked from her son to Chris. "Well, let's get you two out of your wet coats and boots, then you can fill me in on the rest."

Ten minutes later, she had several candles lit, found the flashlights, hung both coats on the back of chairs to dry, made hot cocoa for all of them, and found a bowl of water and some shredded turkey for the canine visitor. The storm had built steam and pounded on the outside of the little house. The windows rattled, and the electricity remained off.

"So, I don't know much about animals, but this little lady looks ready to become a mother any minute. Do you know anything about puppies or delivering them, Chris?" Lana sat on the floor next to the dog and rubbed her back.

"Not on your life."

"Teacher said most animals know what to do when they have young," Sam chimed in. His hot chocolate mustache added a whimsical touch. "And we should give her a name so we don't just keep saying *she*."

Chris looked at her with a smile. "Quite a kid you have there. Wouldn't let me drive him anywhere since I was a stranger. Smart. Any name ideas for her?"

She shook her head. None of this felt real. A snowstorm out of nowhere. A dog about to give birth. And the handsome man in her house who'd made her blush that morning.

What are the odds?

Sam plunked his cup onto the table. "How about Sugar?"

Both adults looked at him.

Lana cleared her throat. "Sugar?"

"Yeah, for the dog. 'Cause when I found her, I gave her the sugar cookie I had in my pocket and it made her like me. It sounds funny. I like it." Sam moved onto the floor next to Lana and the dog.

The dog looked at him with adoring eyes and scooted close enough to lay her head on his leg.

"Sugar it is." Lana shook her head. "Don't know what we're going to do, though. We don't have the time or money for a pet. Surely someone is missing this girl."

Chris tipped his head. "I'm not sure. No collar or tag. And although her tummy is obviously bigger because she's expecting, the rest of her is pretty mangy and thin. No offense, Sugar."

Sugar thumped her tail against the floor in response. She rolled onto her side with a whine and panted.

"Um, Sam, why don't you take my flashlight and go see if you can find that old blanket in the bottom of the linen closet?" When Sam was out of earshot, Lana leaned closer to Chris. "I think she's pretty close to having the pups. What do we do? Should we get her to the vet?"

Her stomach dropped, imagining the expense, but Lana would do it if necessary. No way she'd let an animal suffer.

Chris watched the dog for a couple of minutes, chewing his lower lip. "Well, with the snow and her condition, we probably shouldn't move her unless we really need to."

Lana forced herself to look away. The man was even more distracting in her home than he'd been in the shop earlier that day. The small room seemed even closer with him in it. But...also cozier.

Knock it off, Lana. You have a dog in labor on your floor. Now is not the time to notice Chris.

After Sam returned with the blanket, Lana did her best to make the dog comfortable in the corner near the fireplace.

That way, even if they didn't get electricity anytime soon, she would be warm.

Although with Chris in the room, Lana was certain the temperature had gone up a couple of degrees.

"I'LL SEND Luke a text so he doesn't wonder if I'm in a ditch." Chris sent the bare minimum. Trying to explain this nutty scenario would require a face-to-face.

Will hole-up till snow slows down. Don't wait up.

Chris settled back into a corner of the couch and watched Lana arrange an area for Sugar. Sam hovered, trying to be a help. He was obviously a bright kid, judging by his comments and questions.

"So, can I stay up, Mom? To help Sugar if she needs it?" Sam scratched Sugar's head. The dog seemed to enjoy it, even though she looked away occasionally and breathed heavier.

"Well, bud, maybe for half an hour. You still have school tomorrow." Lana kept her tone soft and even. She seemed to be keenly aware of the dog's mood and stress levels. "Plus, odds are, it could take a while. If something hasn't happened by morning, we'll get Sugar out to Sanctuary so a vet can look at her and make sure everything is okay. Plus, they can scan her for a chip to see if she's just lost."

"Is there anything I can do to help?" Chris leaned forward. "You know, boil water or tear up sheets?"

Lana laughed softly—a gentle sound that warmed him even more than the hot chocolate. He wanted to hear her laugh again. Sometime. "I don't think so."

"So, Sam…" Chris came and stood behind the boy where he sat next to Sugar.

Sam looked up at him. "Sir?"

"You're a hero, you know." Chris nodded toward Sugar. "You and your sugar cookie probably saved her life. Who knows if she could have found a safe place for the night if you hadn't come along?"

Lana looked up at Chris with what appeared to be damp eyes. She cleared her throat and looked away.

Sam seemed to puff up a bit under the praise. "I'm glad I heard her and that you helped us."

After carrying the mugs to the sink, Chris returned to his seat on the couch.

A few minutes later, Lana prompted Sam to get his pajamas on and brush his teeth to prepare for bed. He acted like it was a great adventure with his flashlight in hand.

He came back into the living room for goodnights.

Chris stood when the boy stuck out his hand for a shake. "Thank you for your help, sir."

"Anytime. You did the important parts." Chris watched Sam hug his mom and check on Sugar one more time.

Lana stood and stretched. "Do you mind standing watch while I get Sam tucked in?"

"Go on." Chris smiled. "I've got this."

While Lana took care of Sam, Chris bundled up and took Sugar out to go to the bathroom. Though she lumbered a bit, she took care of business. Once she was settled again on the blanket, Sugar licked his hand. Her eyes seemed to smile.

Get a grip, man. Dogs don't smile with their eyes.

Though for all he knew, maybe they did. But Chris knew for sure that Lana did. He'd caught her doing it a couple of times, though she tried to avoid looking directly at him.

Maybe she's just shy.

Once Lana returned, they both settled onto seats close enough to keep an eye on Sugar. "You took her out? How was the snow?"

"Seems even heavier than when we came in the first time. Still no lights anywhere that I can see."

Lana glanced toward the door. I wonder if I should check on Emma and Mr. Purlman."

"Who are they?"

"Emma owns these cottages and hired me to help keep them up, and Mr. Purlman is our closest neighbor. Sam was coming back from delivering sugar cookies when he heard the dog." Lana worried her bottom lip. "They are both older and alone."

"Tell you what, if the power isn't back on in thirty minutes, I'll go check on them." Chris smiled gently. "That way you don't have to leave your son with a complete stranger."

Lana blushed. Even in the dim firelight, Chris could see it.

"You aren't a complete stranger. Bliss has talked about you several times." Lana laughed softly. "And we were officially introduced. So, I don't consider you a stranger."

Chris wasn't sure why that made him feel good, but it did. Very good.

"So, tell me about your photography. I know you'll be taking care of all the pictures at the wedding." Lana paused to check on Sugar and top off their coffees.

Chris became more animated when talking about his passion for taking pictures. About twenty minutes into sharing about themselves, the lights came on.

Lana stood and turned out most of the lights except one lamp next to the sofa, and looked out the window. "No let-up on the snow yet."

Time slipped past as they shared stories and laughed softly at mishaps they could both relate to. Each took turns sitting next to Sugar. When she dozed off, they returned to more comfortable seats.

Lana could feel the heaviness of her eyelids fighting to stay open.

I really should offer him my room. She'd stay out on the couch to keep an eye on Sugar.

Those were her final thoughts before jerking awake when Chris gently touched her shoulder.

"It's time."

"Time? Sorry, I must have dozed. How long was I asleep?"

"About two hours." Chris smiled. "It's okay. I fell asleep, too."

Suddenly, his first words soaked into her sleep-addled brain. *It's time.* Jerking wide awake, Lana looked toward Sugar. Beside her was a tiny puppy. The tired mama nuzzled and licked her new arrival.

Lana carefully moved next to Sugar, and Chris joined her. Over the next twenty minutes, two more puppies arrived. Three wriggling little ones tried to stay as close to Sugar as possible.

That was amazing. And terrifying. And miraculous.

She and Chris did a quiet high-five that transitioned to him holding her hand for a moment.

"Thanks for letting me be a part of this," Chris whispered.

"Letting you?" Lana smiled. "I think you were roped in by a smart boy. Thank heavens. Doing this alone would not have been fun"

Chris stood. "I hate to bust up the party, but I noticed it had stopped snowing right after I woke up, and before the puppies started arriving."

Lana quelled the flare of disappointment his words brought. She was used to being alone; this would be no different. But for a short time, Lana had enjoyed the feeling of camaraderie that talking and working together with Chris had brought.

It had felt good to have someone help take care of things.

Get over it, Lana. You are more than capable of handling anything.

Helping Chris gather his outdoor gear, Lana kept up a steady stream of smalltalk. That way she wouldn't have to think, or wonder if she'd see Chris again once he went back to New York.

It didn't matter.

Except, it did.

❄❄❄❄

CHRIS CLEARED the snow from his truck and drove away, trying to shrug away the disappointment at leaving.

You didn't even know the woman before you met her at the bridal shop.

Somehow, it seemed longer ago. Being thrown together in the snowstorm, taking care of Sugar and her puppies, and sharing about themselves made Chris feel like he'd known Lana for months instead of hours.

He didn't like that feeling at all.

Except, he did.

❄❄❄❄

THE NEXT DAY was a whirl for Lana. She let Sam stay home from school once he'd woken and been in awe of the new arrivals. She worked from home on more details for Bliss and Luke's wedding, which was now less than two weeks away, and a bit on the February wedding.

Staying busy was good. She shoveled driveways and porches alongside Sam for their neighbors. Together, she and Sam baked batches of sugar cookies to take to them and caught them up on the puppy incident.

Her phone rang late that afternoon, and she almost

dropped it when she heard Chris's voice on the other end. She'd almost made herself believe none of it had actually happened until the deep vibration of his voice against her ear reminded her.

"So how are our puppies?"

Our.

The few minutes of conversation kept Lana smiling all evening.

The next days fell into a pattern of Chris dropping by to help care for Sugar and her puppies. Lana had called Sanctuary, and they'd sent a traveling vet to check on the new family. A scan showed no chip in Sugar. No one had reported a dog matching her description as missing.

Lana opted to keep Sugar and the puppies at the cottage rather than transporting them to Sanctuary. Sam was ecstatic.

The days flew by with putting up a Christmas tree, and caroling with the scout troop. Finally, Christmas Eve and the day of Bliss and Luke's wedding arrived. The puppies were more mobile, but Chris had constructed a temporary corral out of wood just the evening prior to keep them restricted to their corner.

"Sam, can you come take Sugar out one more time before you head to Emma's?" Lana was thankful that Sam wanted to watch some Christmas specials with Emma while Lana took care of the wedding.

After Sam had taken care of Sugar and the puppies, and Lana had helped get him settled at Emma's, she changed into a flowy dress, grabbed the last-minute items, and headed out to the barn at the McPherson ranch to help with the decorating.

Pulling up in front, Lana was pleased to see the caterers unloading their items at the side door and directly into the temporary kitchen staging area.

"Lana!" Bliss hurried out the door, still in jeans and a flannel button-up shirt. "I'm so happy you're here."

Grabbing her hand, Bliss didn't slow down long enough for Lana to respond, but pulled her inside. At least it was much warmer than the outside temperature.

Lana stopped inside the doors and stared. The large, rough space was being transformed into a wonderland by several women. White fairy lights, yellow roses, daisies, and tulle softened the entire space, adding a dimension of shimmer that softened all of the rough edges.

A fully decorated tree occupied a corner next to the arched wooden trellis that was intertwined with more lights. It added a festive touch to the space.

Lana laughed. "It looks like you guys have done a ton of stuff—let me put my things somewhere so I can help with the rest."

"Luke and Chris are here to help with manual labor."

At the mention of Chris's name, Lana felt heat creep into her cheeks. She forced herself not to look around to see if he was nearby.

"Speaking of Chris, it's been nice that the two of you have been able to spend so much time together taking care of the dogs." Bliss didn't miss anything. "I never would have figured him for the nurturing type, but you...I mean the puppies...must bring it out in him."

"We...I...he's a nice guy," Lana muttered, avoiding Bliss's gaze.

Bliss focused on Lana. Facing her directly, she took her hands. "I've seen the two of you together. You stare at each other when you think the other isn't looking. Why do you find it hard to believe that he might be interested?"

Lana gave a small smile. How could she possibly explain all the reasons for trying to maintain her distance from the man? She was working two jobs, plus raising a young boy.

Those things needed to be her priority. Her track record with choosing men hadn't been stellar so far. Not to mention he was going back to New York soon. The reasons were plenty.

"Oh, Chris is just being nice. Probably feels obligated since he's the one who helped Sam get Sugar into the house before she had the puppies." Transitioning to a quick hug, Lana pulled away. "So, this is *your* day. I'm here to make sure the spotlight is on you and the happenings around the event stay in the background, and that includes me."

Bliss laughed and twirled around with her arms outstretched. "I still can't believe this is going to happen. No one from my old life in Boston would recognize me anymore. Wearing old jeans with goat poop on my boots. About to marry Luke. Thank heavens."

Lana pushed her gently toward the door. "And about to do it wearing flannel if we don't finish decorating and get you and your sisters and mom home to get changed. We have one hour. Let's get on it."

Bliss nodded firmly and the group quickly finished transforming the space amidst much laughter and banter.

After Bliss finally headed home, Lana ran through her checklist and headed into the food staging area to see if there was anything she could do to help the caterer.

An hour later, the guests filled the seats. Lana stood at the back near the makeshift anteroom, created from the tack room, where Bliss and her sisters were making sure everything was perfect with the bride.

Bliss's mom, Jane, and her new husband leaned close together, whispering back and forth. They were obviously still newlyweds. Across the narrow aisle, Luke's grandfather, Milt, sat with his lady friend, Rose.

Lana refocused on her responsibilities instead of the obvious love and caring in the room. Just when she'd straightened her spine, she saw Luke and Chris enter from a side door, each dressed in suits, each laughing about something that must have been said before they entered the room.

Heavens to Betsy.

Despite her attempts to keep perspective when it came to Chris, seeing him again caused a silly grin to lift her lips. She quickly smoothed her expression in case anyone looked back at her.

Bliss's voice sounded near her ear. "He's a sight for sore eyes, isn't he?"

Lana nearly jumped out of her skin. She'd been so focused on *not* focusing on Chris, that the bride had been able to walk right up behind her.

"Your groom, you mean?" Lana helped straighten Bliss's veil while the two sisters made their way up front.

"Yes, for me. Chris for you." Bliss took a deep breath, staring straight at Luke who'd now turned and noticed her standing there. "Let's do this. I'm so ready to be that man's wife."

Lana looked away slowly when her gaze met Chris's. The pull between them had grown stronger each day. Spending time with him had only shown her that he was as solid inside as he was good-looking on the outside.

Signaling the music, Lana listened as the strains of the "Wedding March" caused everyone to turn and look toward the bride. Lana tried to blend into the wall she stood against to ensure the focus was on the bride.

Bliss joined a grinning Luke at the wooden arch. They'd written their own vows, and the words brought both laughter and joyful tears from their audience. Including Lana.

I so want to believe love like that is real. Possible.

Once he had handed the ring to Luke, Chris moved aroundsilently snapping pictures of the happy couple and the people watching the ceremony. Five minutes later, Luke and Bliss were husband and wife, and everyone surged forward to congratulate them.

Lana worked on gathering her belongings since once the reception was underway, she could technically head home. She felt Chris's gaze on her.

Their eyes met and he moved toward her.

"Looks like they are going to have the first dance, then open the floor." Chris continued to watch the happenings, taking an occasional picture. "So, are you going to save me a dance?"

Could I dance with him? Without losing more of my heart?

Wait, what?

But Lana realized it was true. Careful as she was, somehow, this man had slipped past her defenses. But, for whatever reason, it made her happy rather than freaked out.

"How about two?" Lana dared.

Chris stopped taking pictures and smiled at her. "You never cease to surprise me."

Ten minutes later, the first dance was done, and other couples migrated to the small dance floor. It filled quickly. Lana finished putting the last of her items in her oversized canvas bag next to the Christmas tree.

"Are you trying to back out of our dances?" Chris stood behind her, no more camera in his hands.

Lana smiled. "Dance floor looks pretty packed."

"Can you hear the music from here?"

She turned to face him fully. "Yes."

Chris held out his hand. Lana placed hers in it. Slowly, they pulled closer and started moving to the music.

This is worth it.

Even if Chris went back to New York and this was all they had—these two weeks, this dance—Lana was thankful because it made her realize she could still feel. She still wanted the dream. The happily-ever-after.

Chris pulled her closer and tucked her head beneath his chin.

Lana smiled. She might not need a knight in shining armor to save her, but this, she'd take any day.

"You know, I've never been in a town like Dogwood." Chris looked down at her. "And I've never met many women as self-reliant and strong as you. Even in New York City."

"I find that hard to believe," Lana replied. "You're probably itching to get back."

Chris returned her to the cozy position they'd first enjoyed. Finally, he took a breath. "Not as much as I thought I would. Actually, not at all."

"Aren't you eager to get back to your company? Your friends?" Lana waited for his response, not wanting to admit how much it meant to her.

"I pretty much telecommute, and my friends live all over the world. New York is just a city." Chris looked down at her. "This place is special. Luke has been telling me that for years, but I didn't believe him. Now, I do."

From across the room, voices grew louder along with laughter. Someone urged Bliss to throw her bouquet between songs.

Lana didn't move. Didn't want to step out of the circle of Chris's arms.

Bliss's arm arched back, and the lovely bouquet flew over the heads of most. Then, Amber, one of Luke's cousins, ended up with it in her arms. A gasp sounded from the folks around Amber, along with many knowing nods and smiles.

I wonder if she'll be the next bride.

A new song began, and Chris raised an eyebrow. Lana accepted his silent invitation and smiled. Together, they stayed next to the tree and danced.

As Chris directed her around the tree, Lana looked up. They were now on the back side of the large evergreen, out of the view of most of the guests, and directly below the mistletoe she'd noticed earlier.

Yes. No. Please. She wanted Chris to notice it, but also feared he would, because then she'd have to make a decision.

Chris looked up and slowed his movements. "Lana?"

She knew what he was asking, but was she brave enough? Could she risk more of her heart?

Slowly, she stood on tiptoe and placed a soft kiss on his cheek. Chris smiled and placed a gentle kiss on her lips, then continued swaying to the last notes of the song.

"Merry Christmas, Lana."

Lana enjoyed the last moments close to the man who'd stolen her heart. As the music faded, she stepped away and moved back to where her bag waited. "I need to get Sam and help him get ready for Santa. And take care of the puppies." She pulled her coat on. "I'm just thankful we didn't get as much snow as the high country to the northwest of town. That would have made it tricky for folks to get out for the wedding."

Chris helped her wrap a scarf over her hair. "Stay warm. Do you mind if I come by sometime tomorrow? To help with the dogs?"

Lana froze. "I thought you had a flight out first thing in the morning?"

Chris smiled, seemingly embarrassed. "Well, I'm afraid I'm not ready to leave Dogwood yet. Luke has agreed to let me rent his guest house for six months."

There was no way to fight the smile that spread across her face. "So, you like Dogwood, huh?"

"Well, and maybe a feisty little brunette I'd like to spend more time with. And her son."

Lana's heart swelled.

"You're not saying anything, Lana." Chris moved restlessly.

She placed a hand against his cheek. "We'll expect you for our Christmas meal, Chris. We'd be honored to have you."

After final goodbyes to the happy couple and several of the new friends she'd made since moving to Dogwood, Lana let Chris walk her to her car.

He scraped the windows while it warmed up.

Lana rolled her window down when he'd finished. "Thank you."

Chris leaned down. "So, around noon tomorrow?"

She placed her hand on his where it rested on her door. "Promise?"

"I promise. Merry Christmas, Lana." Chris placed one more gentle kiss on her lips.

"Merry Christmas."

Lana drove toward home and her son, knowing that no matter what was under the tree in the morning or on the table at noontime on Christmas Day, this was already the best Christmas yet.

And if her heart was right, the first of many.

A CHRISTMAS CATCH

BY KAREN FOX

GARTH MCPHERSON LOVED CHRISTMAS—THE lights, the music, the decorations, even the chaos. The only thing missing was a fresh coat of snow to cover the town of Dogwood. Well, Christmas was two days away. It could happen. He believed, despite what the weatherman said.

"There." He handed out a candy cane to the last child in the large group around him. "That's everybody?"

Heads nodded. "Thanks, Garth," they said in unison. The kids ran off and Garth smiled.

He kept candy canes on hand as he made his rounds through Dogwood. Most of the children knew it, too. If they found him and said, "Merry Christmas," a candy cane was theirs. Everyone should enjoy this holiday.

Garth squinted into the sun, starting its descent behind the mountains. It would be dark soon. End of shift.

Who was he kidding? It was never end of shift. He loved dogs. He loved cats. He loved all animals. That's why his job was the best one anywhere. Only in Dogwood was the Animal Enforcement position one that people didn't fear, and he got to work with animals. Awesome!

A yip in the distance caught his attention. Garth looked around to see a skinny dachshund dashing into the bushes of a nearby yard. He sighed. Scooter. Again.

The dog had the unique ability to escape from his owner's backyard no matter what Mike Brown did to stop him. Garth usually found the dog twice a week.

He approached the bushes, pulling a dog treat from his pocket. He never left home without them. "Scooter? Come on, boy. Time to go home."

A yip sounded, but the dog didn't appear. Garth squatted beside the bushes and held out the treat. "I have a snack for you." He waved it. With luck, the scent would work its way through the bush.

He heard rustling. "Come on, Scoot," he murmured. He kept his hand extended.

Soon, the dog pushed his head out of the bushes. He glanced up at Garth, and Garth swore he grinned. Scooter knew Garth as well as he knew his owner. Escaping was a game for this dog.

Garth drew the treat a little closer to where he crouched and moved it back and forth. "Come on, Scooter. You know you want it."

The dachshund emerged from the bushes to snatch at the treat, and Garth scooped him up. "Time to go home, buddy."

Garth placed him in the back of his small Animal Enforcement truck. Scooter settled at once on a pillow, still crunching the treat. With a shake of his head, Garth closed the truck doors and moved to the driver's seat.

Mike's house was only a few blocks away. Scooter never strayed far, but he did like straying.

Garth parked in front of the one-story house and was halfway up the sidewalk when Mike opened the front door.

"Thanks, Garth." He accepted the dog. "I swear I don't know how he's getting out. He never does it while I'm watching. I've made sure the fence is secure in the ground. There are no openings he can fit through."

"Let's try something," Garth suggested. The idea had come to him as he drove over. "Put Scooter in the yard and go back in the house."

Mike looked dubious. "I think he's too smart to show us what he's doing."

"We'll see."

Mike entered the house, closing the front door, and Garth moved into position outside the chain-link fence that circled the backyard. He didn't see any way for the dog to get out either. Yet Scooter did. Time and time again.

Once the dog entered the backyard and Mike returned to the house, Garth hunched down just outside the fence. He produced another treat. "Hey, Scooter. Still hungry?"

The dachshund ignored him at first, going to pee on a nearby rock grouping at the opposite side of the yard. Garth waited. This dog was getting out somehow.

"Scooter?" He whistled softly. "Want a treat?" He held it close to the fence, and, slowly, the dog ventured near.

Scooter pressed his muzzle against the fence as if expecting Garth to give him the snack. "Not so easy," Garth said. "You gotta come get it."

He waited. Scooter waited. The dog paced away from the fence and Garth looked away. He could play this game.

After a while, he heard the jingle of the fence. Whipping his head around, he fell back on his rear, laughing. "I'll be."

Scooter was climbing the fence, carefully placing each paw in an opening of the chain-link to propel himself upward. With the speed of his ascent, he'd obviously done this many times before.

"Mike, come look."

Mike must have been listening, because he popped out

through the sliding door. Spotting Scooter, he laughed as well. "That's going to be hard to block."

By then, the dog had reached the top of the fence and dropped to the other side with only a small grunt. Garth pushed to his feet and grabbed Scooter before he could dart away. "You are a scoundrel." He passed the dog over the fence to Mike, then gave Scooter the promised treat.

"It may be time for a wooden fence," Garth said.

Mike grimaced. "I think you're right. Thanks."

When he would have turned away, Garth stopped him. "Wait. I forgot." He pulled a fake holly leaf from his pocket and clipped it to Scooter's collar. "Merry Christmas."

"And a Merry Christmas to you."

Garth whistled "Jingle Bells" as he returned to his truck. Yep, he loved Christmas.

🐾🐾

WHAT MADE people like Christmas so much? Arabella Spinnaker groaned as she picked up the ornaments Duchess had knocked off the Christmas tree. Again.

Glancing around the living room, she sighed. The couch pillows were on the floor. Again.

Bella had worked hard to earn her reputation as a pet-sitter in demand. She not only took excellent care of the pets, but cleaned the house and returned it to the owners usually in better shape than they left it.

Duchess's owners, Greg and Cathy Peterman, were due to return tomorrow night, Christmas Eve. They'd left their eight-month old Bolognese puppy in Bella's care for the past week. The cute puffball was a bundle of energy, chewing her way through whatever she could find—rarely her toys—and racing through the house, leaving destruction in her wake.

Duchess only slept when exhausted, and not nearly long enough for Bella.

She replaced the ornaments and turned to pick up the pillows. Bella loved dogs. She honestly did. But around Christmas, everyone was more hyper, including the animals. Her own family spent more time fighting than anything else over the holidays. And Christmas was the worst. If Bella had her way, she'd skip the entire season.

"Duchess? Where are you, sweetie?" She started following the path of destruction, but paused when the doorbell rang. Oh, her pizza.

She grabbed her wallet from the table near the door and swung open the door. The oversized wreath bounced a few times, forcing the delivery boy to step back.

"Sorry." She pulled some bills from her wallet and held them out. "Keep the change."

The boy took the money and passed over the pizza. "Thanks."

A small blur of white dashed out the door as Bella stepped back. "Duchess! No!"

The young man tried to grab the puppy, but failed. In moments, the Bolognese was out of the yard. Bella dropped the pizza on the table and rushed outside, yanking the door closed after her. "Duchess!"

The puppy enjoyed her walks, but she'd never run off before. Now she ran like monsters were after her.

The delivery boy jumped in his seen-better-days Ford and tried to follow the dog, while Bella ran as fast as possible. She had to catch her.

A couple of houses down, Duchess darted across the road and into a small park rimmed with trees and bushes. In moments, she was out of sight.

The delivery boy stopped his car and rolled down the window. "I can't stay. I'm sorry."

Bella waved at him. "That's okay. Thanks for trying." She hurried into the park, then paused near the tree line. No sign of Duchess. Nothing.

"Duchess. Here, girl." Bella whistled and listened. No response. She spun around, searching in every direction.

How far could a puppy go? With Duchess's energy, she could be across town in an hour.

Bella's heart stuttered. No. She had to find that dog.

Calling out, Bella wove between the trees, but dusk followed her, changing everything to shades of gray. No small, white fluffball anywhere. With a start, Bella realized she'd run out into the winter night without a coat. She shivered, but kept going. She wasn't going back for it now.

What was she going to do? Duchess could get hurt, eaten by a mountain lion, hit by a car... Not to mention the damage done to Bella's hard-earned reputation. She'd never get hired to pet-sit again.

Tears trickled down her cheeks as she emerged on a house-lined street. No sign of the puppy.

"Duchess. Please, Duchess." Bella swiped at her face. Crying didn't help anything. She stopped on the sidewalk, unsure where to go next.

A white truck pulled to a stop beside her and the window rolled down. "Are you okay, Bella?"

Bella blinked. She knew this guy. Garth McPherson. He'd been two years ahead of her in high school. With his tall, lanky figure, everyone had thought him a nerd, but he didn't look like a nerd. He looked like a knight in shining armor. "I...I lost my dog."

Garth reached across to open the door to the passenger seat. "Finding dogs is what I do. Hop in."

What other choice did she have? Bella climbed onto the seat and closed the door.

"What kind of dog is he...she?" Garth asked.

"She."

When Bella faced him, he blinked, then handed her a tissue from the box between the seats. "Don't worry. We'll find your missing pup."

Appreciating the gesture, she dabbed at her eyes and nose. His tone was reassuring. Cold to the bone, she stuffed her hands into her armpits.

Garth turned up the heat. "So, kind of dog?"

"Bolognese. Puppy. Mostly white with black-tipped ears."

"Bolognese, huh?" Garth put the truck in motion. "They kind of look like the tribbles from *Star Trek*, right?"

Bella shrugged. She wasn't sure what he meant. He must have guessed as much from her expression.

"Small, fluffy ball of fur?"

"Yeah, that's her."

"Name?"

"Bella Spinnaker."

He grinned. "That, I know. I meant the puppy's name."

"Oh." Heat rose in her cheeks. "Duchess."

"With a name like that, she has to be spoiled rotten." His good-natured tone took all the sting from his words.

"She is." Bella adored the puppy, but Duchess definitely ruled the Peterman household.

"How long have you had her?"

"A week." When Garth shot her a surprised glance, she continued. "I'm dog-sitting for the Petermans while they visit family."

"Oooh." He frowned. "This is bad."

"I know." Bella's voice wavered. Very bad.

"We'll find her." He drove with purpose.

"Where are you going?"

"The dog park. That's where I'd go, if I was a dog on the loose."

That had to be as good as anything else. Bella had taken

Duchess there on one of their walks. Would the puppy remember how to find it?

Dark had fully settled over Dogwood by the time Garth stopped beside the dog park. No dogs played in the fenced area. Bella's heart sank to her stomach. "She's not here."

"We'll see." Garth jumped from the vehicle and walked along the perimeter. Bella hurried to join him. "We'll see if we can bribe her," he told her. He pulled a dog biscuit from his pocket. "My secret weapon."

"I didn't even think of that." A blast of wind pummeled them, and Bella shivered.

"Hey, where's your coat?" Even as he asked, Garth shrugged out of his thick, dark green parka and wrapped it around Bella's shoulders. His warmth clung to it, along with a slight peppermint scent.

"I just ran after Duchess." She tugged the coat around her. It helped.

"I understand. We'll circle the park and see what we find."

They found a fat lot of nothing. By the time they returned to the truck, Garth looked discouraged. He held the door open for Bella and offered her his hand to step up.

"Oh, gosh, you're freezing," she exclaimed. "Take your coat back."

He shook his head. "I'm fine." He shut her door and went around to climb in the driver's side. "Where are you staying? There's always a chance she returned home on her own."

"I hope so." Bella needed something positive to cling to.

But Duchess wasn't there. Bella called for the puppy, but couldn't find her anywhere nearby. With a lump in her throat, she opened the front door she'd forgotten to lock. Garth followed her in.

He went at once to the back door to peer into the yard. After a few whistles, he gave up and reentered the house. "I'm sorry, Bella."

"What do I do now?"

"Not much you can do now. Dogs are smart. She's probably hunkered down somewhere warm for the night. We'll look again in the morning."

"We?" Bella didn't expect him to continue to help her. He'd already gone above and beyond.

"Of course, *we*." He produced a smile that turned his plain face to handsome. "I have to know she's okay, too."

Bella smiled back. How could she not? Garth radiated an aura of caring that warmed her to her toes. Turning, she spotted the pizza still on the table by the door.

"Want some cold pizza?"

"My favorite."

But they heated up the slices in the microwave while Bella brewed two thick mugs of coffee, then settled at the small in-kitchen table to eat.

"How did you know meat lover's is my favorite?" Garth asked, making quick work of his first piece.

"I didn't." Bella had to grin. "It's mine, too."

He nodded. "Great minds think alike."

Maybe *his* great mind. In high school, he'd been a definite brain—chess club, math Olympics. She'd passed, but barely made it through freshman algebra. "How did you end up being the dog catcher?" she asked. It wasn't a position where she'd expected to find him.

Garth pretended to look offended. "Animal Enforcement, thank you."

She acknowledged his correction with a nod and a smile.

"No one wanted the job," he said. "My dad sits on the city council. When they couldn't find anyone, he mentioned it to me. I agreed to take it if I could tailor it to the way I thought the job should be done."

"How is that?"

"We only lock up an animal when we have to, and then I

take it to Sanctuary. No time limits. I prefer to find the owner and return a pet first. I mean, this is Dogwood. Most of these animals belong to someone."

That made sense. "I like that."

"Me, too." Pizza finished, Garth tossed his paper plate in the garbage and faced Bella. "How about I come by in the morning and we look again?"

Sudden panic flooded her. "The Petermans are due back tomorrow evening."

"We'll find Duchess by then."

He sounded so confident that some of Bella's tension eased. "Okay." She smiled. "I really appreciate your help, Garth."

"I'm happy to give it. What's your cell number?" She gave it to him, and he entered it into his phone. "I'll text you so you'll have mine." He headed for the front door. "Till tomorrow."

Bella watched him drive away. As much as she wanted to keep looking, the cold and dark made it almost impossible. She'd start early tomorrow. With Garth.

Garth McPherson wasn't at all who she thought he was. He'd been labeled a geek in high school, and most girls had avoided him. But he was nice and thoughtful and even good-looking when he smiled. His chestnut-brown hair was shorter now, cut above his neck, and his brown eyes held enough warmth to melt snow. She wouldn't mind looking for Duchess with him at all.

❄️🐾❄️🐾

GARTH PULLED his truck to a stop in front of the Peterman's house the next morning. He was actually looking forward to spending a day with Bella. He'd always thought her pretty in high school with her long blond hair and trim figure, but they hadn't run in the same circles. She wasn't nearly as stuck-up as he'd imagined that crowd to be. Good lesson for him. *Don't label people.* He'd never do that to a dog.

Bella must have been watching for him She ran out of the house before he reached the sidewalk. She greeted him with a bright smile that warmed him to his toes despite the chill in the air. Gray clouds covered the sky, blotting out the sun while the wind blew in cold bursts. Not a great day for Christmas Eve.

"I brought a picture of Duchess," Bella said, waving a five-by-seven photo.

"Great idea." He should have thought of that. "Let's go."

"Where?" Bella climbed into his vehicle before he could open the door for her.

He joined her inside the truck before he responded. "I thought we'd walk around downtown. Someone might have seen her."

Bella nodded. "We have to find her." A hint of panic sounded in her voice.

Garth couldn't stop himself from reaching across to touch her arm. "We'll find her." He wouldn't accept any other option.

Once they reached downtown, he parked and held up a long, hand-knitted scarf that sat on the seat between them. "Want to use this? That wind is cold today."

"What about you?"

Her concern made him smile. "I have a warm coat. I'll be fine." She wore a heavy coat today as well. Good.

"Thank you." Their hands brushed as she took the scarf and she paused, her gaze meeting his.

Did she feel that spark, too? *Hope so.*

She wrapped the scarf around her neck, snuggling into it in a move that made Garth want to share in it. *Enough of that.* They had a dog to find.

The sidewalks were filled with people despite the weather. Probably last-minute shoppers. The shops and streetlights were decorated with festive garlands, bows, and lights. Garth had to smile. He never got tired of seeing it. Christmas carols played on an outdoor system, filling the air with familiar melodies.

He glanced at Bella. She didn't appear to appreciate the season's greetings at all. Probably worried about the puppy.

He led them to an approaching couple. "Hi, Ted. Hi, Gina. Merry Christmas."

They stopped with smiles. "Merry Christmas, Garth. Bella."

Garth motioned for Bella to show the photo. "We're looking for a runaway puppy. Have you seen her?"

They studied the photo Bella had brought and shook their heads. "I'm sorry," Gina said. "We'll call you if we see her."

"I'd appreciate that."

They asked several other folks as they progressed down the block with the same results. No one had seen Duchess.

"She has to be somewhere." Bella wrapped her arms around herself.

"She is." Garth draped his arm around her shoulders and tucked her against his side. She fit as if made for him. "Better?"

"Hmmm."

A subtle lilac scent tickled his nose, disappearing too quickly under the gusts of wind. He could get used to having her by him.

"Garth. Merry Christmas, Garth." Several children of various ages ran up to him. He knew at once what they wanted. Thankfully, he'd filled his pockets this morning as usual.

Digging into the deep pocket of his coat, he pulled out a

handful of candy canes and began to distribute them. "Santa comes tonight, eh?" he asked.

"Can't wait." A boy of about six danced from foot to foot.

"I'm going to get a bike," another boy exclaimed.

"You sure about that?" Garth handed him a candy cane with a wink.

Bella held out the photo of Duchess. "Have any of you seen this dog?"

"I have." A girl, maybe seven, was barely visible in her thickly padded parka. She pushed to the front of the group, her hand out.

As Garth gave her candy, Bella knelt down to face her. "When was that, sweetheart?"

"Not too long ago."

"Where?"

"Over by the big church. It was running on the grass."

The big church? Bella straightened. That had to be the Unity of the Rockies at the end of the next block. "Thank you." She grabbed Garth's arm. "We have to go."

"Sure do." He finished passing out his treats. "Have a Merry Christmas, guys."

"Merry Christmas, Garth." The kids ran off with their candy, and Bella leaned into Garth again. She enjoyed the closeness, especially now that she knew where the peppermint scent came from.

He tightened his hold around her shoulders and they hurried toward the end of the street, toward the Dogwood fountain, now dormant for the winter.

"Do you always do that?" she asked him.

"What? Give away candy?" At her nod, he said, "I love Christmas. It's my way of sharing the joy."

"What makes Christmas so joyful?" She'd never found much to celebrate on any holiday.

"Lots of things. The decorations, the music, the food, the

fellowship." Garth paused to face her. "I take it your Christmas isn't so great."

She shrugged. "My family can ruin any holiday. They tend to argue rather than celebrate."

"I'm sorry to hear that. It should be special. You'll have to spend a Christmas with me."

He said the words casually, but a thrill ran along Bella's spine. She'd actually like that.

"We'd make it fun," he promised. He shot her a warm smile, his brown gaze focused on hers, then nudged them into motion again before she could respond.

Did he mean it, or was he just being polite? Bella wanted to spend more time with him. There were facets to this man she wanted to know about. For now, she contented herself with pressing close to his side, absorbing his body heat.

They turned at the fountain, and reached the Unity Church a few minutes later. The white building wasn't fancy, with only a steeple designating its purpose, but it was wrapped in lights with a full-size manger scene filling half the main lawn. She found the church pretty even when it wasn't wrapped in white lights, but right now all she could focus on was finding Duchess.

She'd spent most of the night worrying about the puppy. It was cold, and the Bolognese was young and careless. Bella's reputation as a pet-sitter didn't matter anymore. Finding Duchess alive and well took priority.

"I don't see her anywhere," she said.

Garth took his arm off her shoulders. She missed it at once. "Let's split up and circle the building. I'll meet you at the back."

"Okay." Tucking her hands in her pockets to keep warm, Bella circled to the right, calling for the dog as she went. *Please, be here, Duchess.* She glanced up at the steeple. *Please, help.*

She looked under bushes as she went, but found no sign of Duchess. The swing set on the playground sat empty, the swings moving in the wind. It appeared desolate and cold, much like Bella felt. Especially when she wasn't around Garth.

Spotting him in the distance, she had to smile. Her heart gave a quick leap. How could she get so attracted to him so quickly?

One look at his face erased her momentary joy. "No Duchess?" she asked.

"I'm sorry."

"She's so young. She couldn't have gone far."

"She's near. I know it."

Bella gave him a sad smile. "I wish I had your confidence."

He pulled her into his arms, against his chest. Her head just reached his shoulder. His heat sent an answering flow of warmth throughout her. "It's almost Christmas, Bella. We'll find her."

The wind buffeted them, but Bella didn't care. She'd stay like this forever, the world and its problems held at bay.

But nothing lasted forever. Garth eased her away and started them walking toward the front again.

"What am I going to tell the Peterman's?" They were due home in just a few hours. Duchess was their family. Even as annoying as the puppy could be, Bella loved her, too. Tears threatened.

"We'll find her," Garth repeated. At the front of the church, he stopped and turned in a circle. "Duchess, come on, sweetie. I have a treat for you." He whistled.

A small sound carried across the yard. Bella looked at Garth in surprise. "Was that—?"

He grabbed her hand and whistled again. "Duchess?"

Again, a yip. Near the manger.

Bella ran toward it, pulling Garth with her. The nativity

figures sat around a wooden manger—cows, sheep, and one donkey surrounding them. But no puppy.

"Duchess, where are you?" Bella cried.

The yip came again, close by. Bella whirled around. The manger. A large light bulb was tucked inside some blankets beside a life-like doll to represent the baby Jesus. Cuddled up next to the light bulb was a fluffball puppy.

"Duchess!" Bella scooped up the puppy who enthusiastically licked her face while squirming in her hold. "You naughty girl." Bella pressed kisses to the top of the dog's head, then beamed at Garth. "We found her."

"Of course." His smile was as broad as hers. He reached in to pet Duchess's head. "You are quite the adventurer, aren't you?"

He magically produced a dog biscuit that Duchess latched onto at once.

"I imagine she's hungry," Bella said.

"Then we'd better get her home."

As they turned toward the car, Bella held the dog away from her. What the...? Duchess had garland wrapped around her foot, and her fur was covered in globs of paint and glitter.

Together, they turned to look at the nativity scene. The decorative gifts the Sunday School children had created and placed around the manger were definitely puppy-chewed.

Garth laughed, his face alight. "It appears someone has been partying."

"I think she's going to need a bath."

"I'll help."

"Thanks." Bella hated the thought of saying good-bye to Garth. Every moment she could keep him around was good.

At the house, Bella gave Duchess a helping of her wet food and watched as she devoured it. "I'll go up and run the tub," she told Garth. "Will you bring her up when she's done eating?"

"Not a problem."

Bella gathered the dog shampoo and brush, and had a few inches of water by the time Garth appeared with the puppy. "Thanks."

"How is she with baths?" He lowered Duchess toward the water.

"She's good, but—" She tried to continue, but he'd placed the puppy in the tub where she immediately started splashing in the water. "But she likes to play."

Water stained his plaid flannel shirt. "So I see." He knelt beside Bella. "You wash, I'll dry."

"Sounds like a deal." Bella applied an aggressive layer of shampoo and lathered Duchess, drenching herself as well. Garth leaned in to help, and soon, he was equally wet.

Laughing, they managed to clean the celebratory trimmings off the puppy, who viewed the entire process as a chance to play and splash. When Garth finally lifted Duchess from the tub, Bella couldn't tell which of them needed a towel more.

She grabbed one for Duchess and wrapped her in it. Bella then snatched another towel from the cupboard and tried to wipe the worst of the water off Garth's face and shirt. To her surprise, the chest beneath the soaked shirt was firm and chiseled. Definitely more to this guy than she'd thought.

Her cheeks warmed as she raised her gaze to his. His slow smile sent her pulse racing. Definitely more.

The sound of the front door opening filtered up the steps as Bella wiped off her own face and clothing.

"Bella? We're home."

Bella's gaze met Garth's in shock. "They're home early."

He grimaced. "Well, Duchess is home. And clean."

How was she going to explain Garth's presence? Well, it

wasn't like they were partying. Before Bella could form an answer, Garth set Duchess down on the floor. The puppy immediately raced down the stairs toward her owners.

With a shrug, he followed. Bella had no choice. She walked down beside him.

"You gave her a bath." Cathy Peterman nuzzled the damp dog in her arms and glanced up as Bella and Garth approached. Her expression changed to one of surprise. "Garth. I didn't expect to see you here."

Bella fumbled for a response. "He...I...we're dating and he came over to help me give Duchess a bath. She got into some decorations." She crossed her fingers behind her back. She didn't want to tell them about the puppy's adventure unless she had to. But what was Garth going to think?

She risked a glance in his direction and found a pleased look on his face. "I hope you don't mind," he added.

"Not at all." Greg extended a hand that Garth accepted. "I understand it taking two to give this young'un her bath." He glanced at their wet clothes. "Maybe raincoats should be involved."

Garth laughed. "Good idea."

"Oh, look." Cathy held Duchess out from her chest. "She has some glitter on her. Did you do that?"

Bella swallowed as she nodded.

"It's adorable. Just right for Christmas." Cathy held the puppy out to Greg, who accepted the furball as Bella released a slow breath.

Garth turned to Bella. "I really need to get going, though."

As he started for the front door, her heart sank. Would she ever see him again? Spend time with him?

At the door, he paused and looked back. "Can I pick you up at five tonight to watch the star-lighting?"

He wanted to see her again! "I...yes."

"Good." He held up his phone as he opened the door, indicating she should text him. "Merry Christmas!"

"Merry Christmas," the Petermans chorused. The door shut after him.

"Merry Christmas," Bella whispered. Maybe it would be.

SHE WANTED to see him again. Garth couldn't stop grinning as guided his car into the front of Bella's townhome. He'd changed into a nice sweater to go with his jeans. Not that Bella would notice beneath his heavy coat. Still, he wanted to look nice for her. Maybe that spark he'd felt hadn't been all on his side.

He knocked on her door, his pulse hammering. Why was he nervous? He usually wasn't nervous around most women. But most women weren't Bella.

She opened the door and greeted him with a smile. She'd changed to a red sweater that hugged her curves. His throat went dry. "Ah, hi." Yeah, an amazing conversationalist. That was him.

"Come on in for a minute. I'm almost ready."

He stepped inside and closed the door behind him. She dashed into the kitchen while he admired her small home. Clean, neat, and welcoming. Just like Bella.

She returned with a foil-wrapped plate. "I made cookies," she said. "To thank you."

"You didn't need to do that." Garth peeked under the foil to see a mound of oatmeal-raisin cookies. "But I'm glad you did. These are my favorite."

"Good." Bella left him holding the plate while she pulled a coat from her closet and slid into it. "Shall we go?"

"Yeah. Yeah." Garth hurried to hold the door open for her,

then made sure it was locked as he closed it after them. When had a date mattered so much? Probably never.

They reached Unity Church in a matter of minutes, and joined the crowd forming around the manger scene. Once dark settled completely, the huge star over the nativity would be lit. He loved watching it every year.

Two children approached him as he entered the crowd, his hand at the small of Bella's back. He couldn't resist touching her, and acting as a guide provided a good excuse. "Sorry, guys," he told them. "I'm not packing tonight."

They shrugged. "That's okay, Garth. Merry Christmas."

"Merry Christmas." He did love this holiday. He glanced at Bella to find her watching the manger.

"I think I'll always have a fond memory for this nativity after that," she said. "Especially the decorations." She nodded toward the damaged gifts that thankfully no one had noticed.

He had to grin. "Me, too." He'd never forget today. Even after decades with her. Was that possible?

He nestled her against his side as the crowd stirred. Excitement filtered through the air. It was time.

"Silent Night" played over loudspeakers as the star flickered on. Its immense light illuminated the crowd that sang along to the familiar carol. Even Bella joined in. Was that a sign?

To add to the holiday magic, snow started falling, light at first, then pouring down in heavy flakes. Perfect! As the song ended and the gathering broke into chatter, Garth faced Bella. "Come spend Christmas with me and my family tomorrow?" It might be too soon, but he knew she was the girl for him. "It tends to be loud and chaotic, but no fighting." He held her gaze, sensing the conflict within her. *Say yes.*

"Won't your mother mind?"

"Not at all."

"If...if she really won't mind, I'd like to come."

"Yes!" Garth swung her around in his arms, then kissed her. Her lips tasted of a unique sweetness that had to be Bella. She responded to him, wrapping her arms around his neck as he drew her close to him.

Oh, yes, he wanted a lot more of this.

Cheers and clapping broke through the cloud that kept him five feet off the ground. He looked around to find Match, a black and white border collie who was known for bringing couples together, circling them, her tail cutting the cold air.

His heart nearly exploded. What more could he ask for? "We have Match's blessing," he murmured to Bella.

The gleam in her eyes answered his. "I'm glad." She leaned so close to his face, he was tempted to kiss her again. "Merry Christmas, Garth."

He did love this holiday.

"Merry Christmas, Bella."

A LETTER TO SANTA

BY JUDE WILLHOFF

GIANT SNOWFLAKES FELL GENTLY from the early evening sky as Julie Donovan locked the front door to Donovan Veterinary Clinic. As usual, she and Boomer, her golden retriever, were the last ones to leave work, but that was no big deal. She loved her job as a veterinarian. Her decision to spend her life helping animals was the best one she'd ever made, and now it had become a satisfying career. She glanced back at the window where she'd left the small tree twinkling, and the lights on around the door with their festive colors.

Only a few weeks were left till Christmas, and the wonder of it came home to her. She loved the town of Dogwood at Christmas time. She exhaled a long, contented sigh as the smell of smoke from the chimneys and the bursting scent of pine from the corner tree lot tickled her nose. She'd looked forward all day to the holiday party at her friend Dyan's house tonight. And to the surprise Julie's twin brother Jack had planned. Dyan was going to be over the moon with Jack's proposal. *I wish I had a special someone to surprise me like that.*

"Boomer, you'll get to see Zoe and Luna dog later," she

told the dog as they walked toward the car. "And you're going to get spoiled rotten by that little girl this weekend." Zoe, the seven-year-old daughter of a fireman, had been told by her dad that she could only have a dog if she proved she could take care of one. Julie had let Zoe come to Sanctuary when she volunteered there, and had taught her how to take care of the dogs up for adoption. Keeping Boomer for the weekend was Zoe's big test. "Boomer, you need to be a good boy and help Zoe out."

Boomer barked in agreement.

Anxious as she was to see Zoe tonight, Julie's thoughts were more on Dan Waters, Zoe's dad. Julie had shared a picnic lunch at Dogwood's Fourth of July celebration with the two of them last summer. Since then, she and the child had become very close. Dan was a widower, raising Zoe alone. He was dedicated to his job and raising his daughter, so he didn't have time for dating. Julie had become friends with them both, but she loved that little girl and wanted to be more than just Dan's friend.

Dan would be at the party. Would tonight be any different? She shrugged. *I'll get to see how Dan acts toward me.*

Julie tossed her long hair over her shoulder. She wasn't used to wearing it down. "Boomer, here's to my plan." She gave him a small Christmas dog biscuit. "Tonight, I will make Dan notice me as a woman, not just as a friend."

Dressed in his colorful red Christmas sweater with white snowflakes, Boomer cocked his head to one side, glanced up at her, and wagged his tail in approval as they made their way down the street.

From Julie's view, the town looked pretty as a postcard—the tree with its star in the town square by the fountain, and the street lamps aglow. Dogwood looked like a Thomas Kincaid painting, all white and snug between the mountains and forest with the glowing holiday lights. The town lifted her spirits. "Boomer, isn't it pretty? Anything can happen during the holidays."

Boomer gave Julie a doggie grin as he trotted beside her.

It was beginning to look a lot like Christmas, and the excitement was contagious. People she met along the sidewalk were smiling as they passed. She loved this time of year with all the colored lights on the houses, the snow, and crackling fires. And the expectant smiles on the faces of the children made her heart do a tumble. No other holiday compared.

"Get in the car, Boomer. We're already late." Julie closed the door behind him and climbed behind the wheel. It wasn't far from her office to the party.

When they drove around the corner, Dyan's house came into view. Julie's heart raced with excitement for her best friend. Tonight was going to be a night to remember.

Dyan had brought the 1896 Victorian back to its former glory in honor of her father, and the house decorations were beautiful. The exterior white icicle Christmas lights had been hung around the tall turret and the eaves of the Victorian home. Green garland with red bows decorated the white wraparound porch, and a huge green wreath with a big red bow and golden sleigh bells hung on the front door. Most everyone was already here. There wasn't anywhere close to park, so Julie parked down the street from the house.

She put Boomer on the leash. The large snowflakes drifted down softly, hitting Julie's face as she took a deep breath in anticipation of the night.

They were enjoying their brisk walk through the snow when Dan and Zoe drove up beside them and slowed. His truck rolled to a stop with the window down. "Hey, pretty lady, going our way?" Dan asked from the driver's seat. Zoe grinned from ear to ear.

Butterflies erupted in Julie's stomach at the sound of his

husky voice. He always flirted with her, but that's as far as it went. "Well, it just so happens, I am." She felt a warm glow flow through her. *Maybe tonight he'll notice me as more than a friend.*

He parked the truck, and he and Zoe got out and walked along with her.

"You look pretty with your hair down and curly. I've never seen it that way," Zoe said.

"Thanks, Zoe. Yeah, I usually wear it up at work." She touched her blond hair.

"I agree with Zoe, it looks good." Dan smiled. "Are you ready for this evening?"

"Oh yes, I think it's going to be fun."

"Then let's get in there. We're running a little late."

Zoe bubbled with excitement. "I'm so happy you're letting Boomer stay with me this weekend. I'll take good care of him, I promise," Zoe said and hugged Boomer to her side. The dog was eating it up with a silly grin on his face.

"I'm sure you will." She couldn't help but return the little girl's happy smile.

As they arrived at the doorstep, Dyan opened the door. "I'm glad you're finally here. Come in and make yourselves at home."

"Dyan, the house looks beautiful." Julie glanced around the open living room. Cozy furniture filled the area and a fire burned in the gas fireplace.

"Thanks, I'm happy at how it's all turned out." Dyan turned back to Zoe. "We really need your help decorating the tree."

Zoe smiled, showing one front tooth missing. "We have one at school, and I'm a good tree decorator. My teacher said so."

Jack took Julie's coat. "Sis, you look pretty tonight."

"Thanks, big brother." After all, he was five minutes older than her. "Is everything ready?" she whispered in his ear.

"Yes, I'm just waiting for the right moment. I think I'll do it in front of the tree after we get it all decorated."

Julie gave her brother a one-armed hug as they walked into the living room. "That's perfect. You're going to knock her socks off."

"Rudolph the Red Nosed Reindeer" played on the stereo, and the house was filled with Christmas music and laughter. The scent of the freshly cut tree smelled wonderful.

Tree decorations lay on a side table. Dyan had an ornament made for each guest with their name and the year written in fancy script on the swirled gold and purple globes.

"She's thought of everything," Julie commented.

Jack beamed. "Just about. There are snacks and pizza in the dining room from Bar Pietro. Drinks are in the refrigerator and on the counter."

As always, Boomer tilted his head and looked up at her with that knowing look in his eyes. "I swear you are the smartest dog I know. You know we're talking about food, don't you? No worries, I'm sure Dyan has some treats for you, too. Later."

The dog tilted his head, listening as if he understood, and as soon as Julie let him off the leash, he ran to play with Luna, Dyan's golden retriever.

Dan and Jack went off together, chatting away. They'd become good friends. Since one was a fireman and the other a policeman, their jobs brought them together a lot.

Zoe bounded over to check out the ornaments, and Julie had to smile. Dan was doing a great job raising her as a single father. After his wife died in a car accident when Zoe was only five, he moved to Dogwood because it was too painful to live in the home without his wife. He had told Julie too many memories lived there. She admired Dan for being so dedicated to his child.

Julie placed her ornament on the tree while she chatted with some of the other guests. Dan and Zoe approached.

"I want to put mine next to yours," Zoe said, and added her ornament, then smiled up at Julie.

"Of course, sweetie. It looks beautiful." Julie stood back and looked at the huge tree standing in the turret room of the newly remodeled Victorian home. To a child, it must look like something out of a fairy tale.

Zoe glanced at her dad. "It's going to be the best Christmas ever."

Julie's heart ached at the child's words, knowing how much they must mean to her father.

"The best Christmas ever.... Because of this giant tree, huh, Zoe?" Dan teased his little girl and grinned at Julie.

Julie noticed there was something different in his eyes tonight. A twinkle that she hadn't seen there before. It must be the season.

"I have something for you," Zoe said with excitement and handed Julie a small black box.

"What's this?" She held the box in her hand, curiosity building inside her. She was blown away by the unexpected gift. "It isn't Christmas yet."

"Open it." Dan smiled at her. "It's an early Christmas present from Zoe."

"I like spending time with you and Boomer and all the other dogs." Zoe smiled that impish grin and looked back at the tree.

Julie inched the purple bow from the box and lifted the top. A golden Christmas tree with different colored stones for ornaments lay nestled in the purple tissue paper. Reading the words written on the back brought a tear to her eye. It said, "Julie, my best friend in Dogwood. Merry Christmas, 2018."

"I love it. I'll cherish it forever, and put it on my tree." She leaned down and gave Zoe a hug and kissed her on the cheek. "Thank you."

She glanced up at Dan, and noticed a tender look in his eyes. Who knew, maybe she had a chance to break the ice with him, too.

Zoe's eyes gleamed with pride. "I'm getting a dog for Christmas." She glanced up at her dad.

"Now, Zoe, we've talked about that. It's not for sure. You have to prove to me you can take care of Boomer first."

"I know, but Boomer is easy to take care of, so my dog is on the way with Santa. I just know it."

Julie glanced at Dan. For Zoe's sake, she hoped it all worked out.

Zoe looked up at her dad and an odd look came on her face. Julie wondered what the child was thinking.

Dyan came over to them. "It's kind of crazy here tonight, I wanted to check on you all."

"No worries, we'll take care of ourselves," Julie said.

Jack came by. "Dyan, sit and take a break," he insisted. "I'll bring your drinks in a minute." He winked at Dyan. "I know what you both drink, and I bet I know what Miss Zoe likes, too." Jack grabbed Dan to help.

Julie and Zoe sat together on the loveseat and looked around the room. "Your tree is huge. I see why you wanted help trimming it," Julie said.

"We're getting our tree tomorrow after my dad looks at a house to buy us," Zoe said, and smiled up at Dyan. "He said you're his realtor."

"Yes, I'm your realtor. Your daddy is looking for the perfect home for you," Dyan said. "But we won't take long, so you'll have plenty of time to pick up your tree."

"Can you find us a house with a blue spruce tree in the yard?" Zoe asked.

Dyan shrugged and looked at Zoe curiously. "Maybe."

That was an odd request from a little girl. Julie watched her face, wondering what was on her mind. *With all those long blond curls and big blue eyes, Zoe's going to be a heartbreaker one day. Dan is going to have to get a broom to sweep the boys away.*

Dyan pushed a wayward strand of blond hair behind Zoe's ear. "You know, Julie." Dyan glanced between them. "With your hair down, you and Zoe look a lot alike."

Zoe smiled a crooked grin. "That makes me happy 'cause we're best friends."

"Yes, we are, sweet pea, and don't you forget it." Julie gave her a hug. *This child is so precious.*

Zoe looked toward Dyan. "Santa needs to know where everyone lives, and your house glows, so I know he can find you."

"Yes, it's very important that Santa find us," Dyan said seriously.

"I don't think Santa will be able to find me this year. Since we moved from our house in Colorado Springs, I don't think he knows where we live."

"Oh, honey, I'm sure he does." Dan and Zoe had moved to Dogwood over two years ago. "Did you write Santa a letter?" Julie asked, curious why Zoe seemed so concerned.

"I finished it today at school. I've got it in my pocket." She patted her jeans and sighed. "But I don't know if he'll get it."

"Why not?"

"Mommy told me to clip it to the blue spruce tree in our backyard every year, and the red bird of Christmas would find it and take it to Santa." Her lip quivered. "We don't have a blue spruce tree at our apartment. The bird won't know where to find my letter."

So that was why she wanted a house with a spruce tree....

Zoe looked forlorn. "The last couple of years, she didn't find it. It has to be a blue spruce tree, 'cause the red bird really likes those. I found my letter on the ground last time." She sniffled. "It falled off and somebody stepped on it."

Julie's heart nearly broke. She could only imagine how crushed Zoe must've felt. *This Christmas has to be different. I'll make sure of it.* No child should have to go through that.

"Did you tell your daddy? I'm sure he could help you," Dyan said.

"No, he's got a lot of work stuff on his mind and besides, that was just for Mommy and me." A tear slid down her cheek. "I miss my mom."

Julie hugged Zoe to her side. "I know you do, honey." Julie tipped up Zoe's chin and looked her in the eye. "I'm sure that red bird will find your letter this year."

"Do you really think so?"

Julie gave her another hug. "You can count on it. That bird will find you this year. She hasn't forgotten."

She smiled at Julie and Dyan. "Don't tell anyone, but I asked Santa for a present for my daddy this year. I want Santa to bring him someone who makes him happy, like my mommy used to do."

Julie swallowed the huge lump in her throat. This little darling was putting her dad ahead of her own Christmas wishes. What a generous little sweetie. *Could I make Dan happy?*

"We'll keep your secret," Dyan said. "Are you hungry? We have pizza and some other snacks. And, after dinner, we'll put some more ornaments on the tree. I have some special ones just for you to hang."

Boomer kept pushing Zoe's hand with his nose. "Cool, but now I want to go play with Boomer and Luna."

"You go play, and let me know when you get hungry," Julie said.

Zoe ran off and picked up a rubber toy chicken and held it out to Boomer. Boomer tugged and played along.

ZOE PLAYED with Boomer and his toy, but talking to Dyan and Julie about the red bird and the spruce tree made her think. Even if Daddy found a house that had a blue spruce in the backyard, it wouldn't be in time to get her letter to Santa. That was still a problem. She couldn't have the same thing happen as last year. This year, her wish was too important. Daddy hadn't been happy much since Mommy went up to heaven, and Santa was her only hope. But how could she make sure her letter was delivered this year?

She patted the letter in her jeans pocket and put her hand on Boomer's back as she walked toward the back of the house. Maybe she could find Luna to play with Boomer while she tried to figure out what to do.

DYAN GLANCED AT JULIE. "I see you and Zoe have become close."

"She's easy to love, but I have to watch myself before I get too involved. Dan still isn't over losing his wife. We're friends, but I don't know if it'll ever be more than that. But I'd do anything for that little girl." She sighed.

"I know Dan has his issues, but I see chemistry between the two of you. Grief is different for everyone—you just have to give him time."

"Oh, he can have all the time he needs. There's nobody else I'm interested in." She smiled. "Looks like Dan will need to find a red bird of Christmas for Zoe, or at least a blue spruce tree. I didn't even know there were red birds at Christmas."

"Me either, but I bet there'll be one at Dan's house this year," Dyan said with a smile.

"Of course. I'll make sure of it."

Jack brought Dyan and Julie each a glass of wine.

"Sis, you look especially pretty tonight," Jack said as he handed her the glass.

Embarrassed in front of Dan, she blushed. *Note to self. I should wear my hair down more often.*

Jack and Dan walked away with their beers in hand.

"Jack's right. You do look lovely in that red cashmere sweater. It's your color," Dyan said.

"Thanks. My goal was to get Dan to notice me tonight, and apparently everybody is noticing what a slob I've been, always wearing my hair in a ponytail." She rolled her eyes.

"I'm sure Dan's noticed you." Dyan smiled. "I've noticed him, noticing you, when you aren't looking." She laughed. "I have to go check on the snacks. I'll be right back."

"No worries, I know you have to mingle. I'll be around."

Dyan smiled. "You're the best. You go and have fun. Track that Dan down."

"Sure, I'll do that," Julie said, as she watched the party going on around her. *Was Dan really watching me? Maybe there's hope yet.* Her heart did a little happy dance. She was thrilled Jack and Dyan had found each other again, and this was what she wanted in her life—a home and someone to love. *The bottom line is, I'm tired of being alone.* She got up and went to check on Zoe.

Zoe was on the back porch in the play area Dyan had made for the dog. Snuggled on the couch with a dog on either side, she seemed very content.

"Hey Zoe, how are you doing?" Julie asked.

"We're having fun. Boomer and Luna are the best."

"I'm glad you're having fun, but you can come out front with the adults. They'd like to spend time with you, too."

"That's what Daddy said, but I'd rather play with the dogs."

"That's okay, sweet pea, if that makes you happy. Some days, I feel that way myself. Just know we'd like you out there with us, too."

"Okay."

As Julie came back into the living room, she watched Jack put his arm around Dyan. It must be about time for the big event. She could hear them talking.

"We're going to have many nights like this in our future," Jack said.

"Yes, my life is so full right now, I could almost burst. It's fun to have all our friends and family together in our home."

I want that kind of love.

"Could I have everyone's attention, please?" Jack asked. "I want to make a toast to my lovely Dyan and her new home."

Dyan glanced at Jack and raised her eyebrows as everybody looked on. "What's going on?"

Jack cleared his throat. "As you know, Dyan and I have known each other since sixth grade, and we've had our ups and downs in our relationship."

Everyone laughed.

"Well, I know in my heart she is the only woman for me, and I'd like to make it official." He got down on one knee in front of the Christmas tree, facing her. Jack's eyes glowed with pure love as he spoke to Dyan.

Julie knew what was coming. Dyan had hoped Jack would give her a ring for Christmas, but this was even better, proposing in front of all her friends. It had been so hard to keep this secret from her best friend.

Jack gazed into her eyes. "Dyan, you know I've loved you since the day I pulled your pigtails and you chased me around the playground. That day, I somehow knew that one day you would be my wife." A murmur of laughter ran through the crowd.

He was serious for a moment. "We've been through a lot, and now we know without a doubt that we belong together, and want to have a family of our own. You are the woman of my heart. I want to spend the rest of my life with you."

He gave Dyan that lopsided grin that Julie knew always melted Dyan's heart.

"Will you marry me?" He held out the opened ring box. A wide golden band with a large diamond surrounded by a circle of smaller diamonds winked as it lay nestled in the box.

She looked at Jack with shimmering tears of joy in her eyes. "Yes, Jack, I'll marry you."

He put the ring on her finger and kissed her.

Everyone clapped and cheered for the happy couple. Julie rushed forward and hugged her brother and Dyan. "I'm so happy for you both. Congratulations."

"Thanks, sis. You were right all along about us belonging together," Jack said. "I should listen to you more often."

"Where's my phone?" Julie said. "I need to get this recorded, because I'll probably never hear those words come out of your mouth, again."

He laughed, and everyone surrounded Jack and Dyan, congratulating the two of them. Julie was happy for them, but couldn't help but envy what they had together. She would just have to be satisfied with sharing their joy.

🐾🐾🐾

ZOE PEEKED down the hallway at the grownups enjoying the Christmas party. "They won't miss me." She frowned at the dog. "Come on, Boomer. It's stopped snowing, and we have to go while Daddy is busy." She'd take Boomer with her and show her daddy she could take care of a dog. She patted Boomer on the head. "We can take my letter to the blue spruce tree and be back before the party is over."

Zoe couldn't find Boomer's leash, so she tied a long wide piece of red ribbon around his collar. "It's okay, boy. I've got a flashlight and snacks in my coat pocket for both of us. I know the way to our old house. We'll just put the letter to Santa on the blue spruce tree, and then we'll come right back here before anyone knows we're gone."

Boomer pulled against the ribbon and tried to tug her back inside the house.

Luna whimpered as they went out the back door.

"Sorry, Luna, but this is a trip just for Boomer and me. Come on, boy, we have to go while Daddy's busy." She pulled the reluctant Boomer along with her and giggled as she headed out on her special mission.

❖ ❖ ❖ ❖

As JULIE WATCHED Jack and Dyan enjoy what had turned into their engagement party, she saw Dan walk up to Jack, a look of deep concern on his face. Julie made her way to him quickly.

Her heart jumped to her throat as she overheard his words. "Jack, I'm sorry to disrupt your party, but I can't find Zoe." Dan's voice was laced with panic. "The last time I looked in on her, she and the dogs were taking a nap. I've looked everywhere. She's missing. I need help."

Panic flared inside her. "Let's go through the house from top to bottom. There are a lot of places to hide," Julie said. "Maybe she fell asleep somewhere."

"Her coat and Boomer are gone," Dyan said. "Luna is out there whimpering at the back door. She went out that way."

"I just don't get it. She was so excited about coming to the party. Why would she do that?" Dan ran a hand through his hair and ran to the back door.

"I'll call the police station. They'll start looking for her. She's on foot, so she couldn't have gotten far," Jack said. "Get our coats and we can follow her in the snow. We'll find her."

Dan grimaced. "I know, but my worry is that the highway runs right through town. What if a stranger picked her up?"

Jack gave him a stern look. "Let's not go there. Maybe she just walked home. Your apartment is close by."

❅ ❅ ❅ ❅

ZOE AND BOOMER trudged alongside the highway. Dragging her footsteps, she thought they should be in Colorado Springs by now. The snow was getting harder to walk in, and it was up over her boots, nearly to her knees. She felt like they had been walking forever, and she was cold and tired.

"Boomer, it can't be much farther. We'll be there soon." She gave him a piece of a cookie. "I'm sorry it's taking us so long to get to my old house. I promise I'll get you some water to drink when we get there."

The dog ate the treat, then tugged on the long ribbon and pulled Zoe away from the road, but a semi-truck barreled by, splashing them both with dirty, snowy water from the road.

Shivering with cold, Zoe stood rooted to the spot. Tears ran down her face, mingled with the streaming gunk from the road. *I want my daddy.*

Boomer snuggled next to her side and pushed her farther away from the road.

She hugged his neck and wiped her tears in his fur.

Just then, a shiny red sports car pulled off the highway and stopped beside them. An older man with round, wire-rimmed glasses, long white hair, and a white beard opened his passenger door.

Knowing about stranger danger, Zoe's first thought was to run away. She brushed the dirty water from her face, but she stood still, wet and freezing in the chilly night air, too tired to move.

"Hi there, Boomer, you're looking festive tonight with your pretty red ribbon," the man said, and gave her a pleasant smile. "And Miss Zoe, where are you two going?" He gave Boomer a Christmas dog biscuit.

Boomer tugged at the ribbon to get to the treat.

Zoe knew she wasn't supposed to talk to strangers, but he knew their names. "How do you know our names?"

"I know many names. I've known Boomer since he was a puppy. I was there when he was born. His mother is a very good dog."

How could that be? She looked closer at the man and noticed a twinkle in his eyes. He was wearing jeans, a red shirt with suspenders that had candy canes and Christmas trees on them, and cowboy boots. He must be a nice man. All the guys she and her dad knew who wore cowboy boots were nice to her. "I like your cowboy boots."

"Thanks, Mrs. Cla...my wife gave them to me. She said when I come to the West, I should dress like the cowboys. She'd like you." He smiled at her and the dog. "And where are you going?"

The words gushed out of her mouth. "I'm going to my old house in Colorado Springs. We're taking my Christmas letter to put on the blue spruce tree so the red bird can take it to Santa."

"Well, it just so happens that Colorado Springs is where I'm going. I'd be happy to give you both a ride."

"My daddy told me not to ever get in a car with a stranger."

"Your daddy is a very smart man, but I think he would want you to come with me. It's getting colder outside, and the temperature is dropping. I know you're both wet, cold, and tired."

"Yeah, we are." She stood, undecided, but Boomer jumped up into the car seat, pulling Zoe along with him.

Julie said Boomer was a good judge of people, so this man must be okay.

She shivered and climbed into the front seat. Boomer sat between her and the man. "We don't want to freeze, so we'll come with you." The heated seats felt good, and she was finally able to relax. She patted Boomer's head and saw his tongue hang to one side as he laid his head in her lap. "Boomer, I'm sorry I made you walk so far," she whispered in his ear.

"Boomer is tired, but I can assure you he'll be okay. He's a good boy," the man said.

"I sure hope so." She sighed.

"Don't worry. He's fine."

"Okay." She looked out the window at the highway. "This sure is a pretty red car."

"Thank you. I kind of like her. I call her Prancer. You know, like the reindeer."

"That's so cool that you name your car." Zoe laughed and snuggled with Boomer, happy to be warm and riding to her old home.

"What's your address in Colorado Springs?"

"Seven-sixteen Holly Lane. I used to live there until my mommy went to heaven." She looked down at the floor. "I miss her."

"I know she misses you, too, but I don't think she would want you walking along the highway by yourself, do you?"

She frowned. "No, but I didn't think it was this far, and I have to get my letter to the blue spruce tree or the red bird won't be able to find it to take to Santa." Her chin stuck out in determination as she pulled the letter from her pocket. "I have to put it on the tree just like me and my mommy did, so Santa will know what I want him to bring my daddy."

"Oh, you have that kind of problem. I do understand. What do you want Santa to bring your daddy for Christmas?"

"I want him to bring him someone he can like as much as my mommy. We both miss Mommy, but Daddy needs someone to make him laugh again."

"That's a nice thing to ask for your dad. And what do *you* want for Christmas?"

"I'd like a puppy to love and be my very own." She yawned.

"I see. Puppies are special animals. Do you think you can take care of a puppy?"

"Oh, yes. My friend Julie taught me how. It would be wonderful if I had one of my own to love and take care of. I'd clean up after it and take it for walks and make sure it had plenty of food and water."

"It sounds like you're ready to own a puppy." He touched his finger to the side of his forehead. "I see a little basset hound in your future. And her name is Molly. Would you like that?"

"I'd love that, but after tonight, I don't know if I'll ever get a puppy. Daddy is going to be so mad at me."

He smiled. "Your daddy loves you, and will be happy to see you. Why don't you rest now, and if you fall asleep, I'll wake you when we get to your house. It isn't far, now."

"Okay." All of a sudden, Zoe could barely keep her eyes open. She was tired from all the walking and adult conversation. Boomer let her lean against his side as he watched the gentleman driving the car.

She heard the man whisper. "Sleep, my child. You're both safe with me. Ho, ho, ho. Onward, Prancer."

Zoe drifted off to sleep.

❄ ❄ ❄ ❄

AT THE POLICE STATION, Julie stood next to Dan and Dyan. "Dan, Jack is doing everything he can to find her," Julie said, as she held back the moisture in her eyes. She grasped his hands. "I love her too, and I'm here for you."

"Thanks, Julie. That means a lot."

It was obvious he was worried, and she was too. She silently prayed for Zoe's safety as she saw Jack coming toward them with a scowl on his face. She knew it wasn't good news.

"Dan, I'm sorry, we've scoured the town and there's no sign of her," Jack said. "Do you have any idea where she might have gone?"

He dropped Julie's hands. It was if a part of her heart was ripped away. She wanted to comfort him, but now wasn't the time.

"No, she's never done anything like this. I thought she might have decided to walk home, but she hasn't been there. My neighbor is keeping an eye out in case she shows up." He paced the floor. "Jack, what if someone picked her up?"

"We have an alert out for her. Everyone in Dogwood is looking for her."

"I know, but it's after dark and freezing out there. We've got to find her." He shook his head. "She never did anything like this in the Springs."

The Springs... In sudden realization, Julie stepped forward. "I don't know why I didn't think of it earlier, but I might know where she's gone."

"Where?" Dan asked.

She repeated the story Zoe had told her and Dyan at the Christmas party. "Maybe she thought she could walk to Colorado Springs to her old house to put her letter on that tree. Being so young, she wouldn't realize how far it is."

Dan groaned. "Oh, God, I should've known she cared so much about that Santa letter. She told me she finished it, and that was all she could talk about. I thought she'd give it to me to mail to Santa. I never dreamed she'd try to take it back there." He headed toward the door. "It's a scary thought, but it's the only idea we have."

"I'll alert the Colorado Springs PD to keep an eye on the residence for her," Jack said. "And you're in no shape to drive. Let's take my patrol car. We can watch along the side of the road for her on the way. The rest of the department will keep searching here."

Jack turned to Dyan and Julie. "It might be best if you keep looking around town. This is a long shot, and she still might be here."

"No way—we'll follow you in my car. I know she's going to be there, and I need to be there for Dan and Zoe." Julie stood firm, but gave Dan a hug. "It's going to be okay. We'll be right behind you."

He nodded and hugged her back. As he hurried out the door, she saw moisture glistening in his eyes. It about broke her heart. The man had suffered enough. He'd already lost his wife. He couldn't lose Zoe, too. *God, please bring Zoe back to us.*

Julie and Dyan followed them out of the parking lot. They had lights and sirens blasting, but Julie would keep up with them. She concentrated on her driving.

"They'll find her, Julie. I know they will," Dyan said.

"That's what I'm praying for. And I know Boomer wouldn't let anything happen to her if he can help it." A tear slid down her cheek.

"None of that. We're thinking positive here. She's going to be okay," Dyan said.

"You're right. Let's get there."

🐾 🐾 🐾

ZOE HEARD a voice calling to her from far away, tugging her awake.

"Miss Zoe, we're here at your old house. It's time to wake up."

She glanced over and saw the old man smile at her. She stretched and remembered where she was.

"Now, what do you have to do here? There's nobody at home." He grinned at her. "I'd be happy to help you."

Zoe peeked out the car window. It was her house. Images of her mommy flashed before her eyes and her heart hurt all over again. "I need to go to the backyard."

"Then that's what we'll do," he said.

"There's a blue spruce tree there that I have to clip my letter to so the red bird of Christmas can take it to Santa. But I forgot to bring a clip." Her voice cracked.

"What a wonderful idea. I happen to have a special item for you to put it on the tree with." He pulled something from his pocket. "I'll walk back there with you."

"Okay," she said. "I'm glad I met you."

"I'm happy I met you, too, sweet child. Everything is going to be okay."

Together, they got out of the car and walked toward the blue spruce tree. Zoe stood in front of the tree, shivering, with Boomer beside her.

The man dressed in red stood next to her. "Here you go, put your letter on the tree with this." He handed her an angel-shaped clip. "I'm sure the red bird will get it to Santa.

But you know Santa will always be able to find you, no matter where you live."

Maybe. But Zoe wanted to be sure about this Christmas wish. When Zoe put the clip on the tree, she had the warmest feeling inside. A warm golden light surrounded her, and, suddenly her mommy stood in front of her.

She couldn't believe it. "Mommy," she cried in excitement.

Her mother hugged her and placed a soft red blanket around her shoulders, making her feel warm all over.

"Zoe, I'm always with you," Mommy said. "With my blessing, someone is coming to make you and your daddy happy." She hugged her once more. "I have to go. I love you." She smiled and slowly disappeared.

As Zoe stared where her mother had been, now all she could see was the tree. The Santa letter was gone. Her mother was gone. And so was the man who'd helped her.

"Mommy, don't go," Zoe cried out. On her knees in the snow, she grasped the soft red blanket tight with one hand, and held golden jingle bells in her other hand. Where did those come from? Boomer stood beside her with the same type of bells around his neck. She held on to Boomer and hugged him. She glanced back at the tree. Yes, the letter was gone. She hadn't imagined it, and the man had given them the bells. Could it be?

"Boomer, that was my mommy...and Santa." But now she was all alone. "I want my daddy." A tear slid down her cheek as she snuggled against Boomer and shook the jingle bells. "Maybe he'll hear the bells and come find us," she whimpered into Boomer's neck.

At that moment, a police car with flashing lights pulled into the driveway, another car right behind it.

She saw her daddy jump out of the car and run toward her. And Julie ran from the other car.

❧ ❧ ❧ ❧

THANK GOD, Zoe was safe. Julie rushed toward Zoe, never so happy to see anyone in her life.

Dan dropped to his knees and gathered his daughter tightly.

Zoe hugged him back, saying, "Daddy, Mommy and Santa were here. Mommy said she loves me, and is always with me, and somebody nice is going to make us happy." She looked at Julie. "Santa took my letter. Mommy gave me this blanket, and Santa gave me the bells."

"Oh, sweetheart, don't you ever do that again. I was so scared." He hugged her close and the bells jingled. "I heard the bells. Where did you get those?"

"I told you. Mommy and Santa were here." She yawned. "I was tired, and we were wet and cold. He took care of me and Boomer. I clipped my letter to the tree with the angel clip. Mommy was here, and she put this big warm blanket around me and held me in her arms. Then she disappeared.

"Santa took my letter and left me those bells." She sniffled. "I'm sorry I left the party, Daddy. I love you. I know Mommy is watching over me, and Santa can find me now." She held her father tight and looked up at Julie. "Boomer is the best dog ever. I took good care of him."

"I know you did, sweetheart. Boomer is fine. He just needs a bath." And so did Zoe. Julie laughed.

As Dan tucked the blanket around Zoe, Julie heard a whimper. Dan peeled the blanket back, and inside its folds was a tiny basset hound with big brown eyes and long floppy ears.

Julie took the puppy from Dan. "Zoe, look what your Daddy found in the blanket." She exchanged a wondering glance with Dan. "Did Santa leave this for you?"

Zoe reached for the puppy, delight shining in her eyes.

"It's Molly. Santa said I'd have a puppy named Molly. Daddy, can I keep her?" Zoe held the puppy with both hands as her father picked her up and carried her toward the car. "She's so cute." The puppy licked her hand. "Daddy, she likes me."

"Who am I to go against Santa? Of course you can. You've earned her by taking such good care of Boomer."

Dan shot a bemused glance at Julie. "I don't understand what's happened here, but my baby is safe. That's all that matters." He shook his head. "Zoe has a blanket from heaven and a puppy from Santa. I've never seen anything like it, but I'm grateful." Tears of joy streamed down his cheeks as he held his child.

"It's the magic of Christmas," Julie said in wonder.

He set Zoe in the cruiser and turned to Julie. "Thank you so much for being there tonight. If it hadn't been for you, we wouldn't have found her."

Julie started to protest that she'd done nothing, but Dan enveloped her in a hug.

She suddenly felt wrapped in a warm cocoon of euphoria. Stunned, she hugged him back. "You know I'd do anything for you two," she whispered instead.

He pulled back and cleared his throat. "Then would you like to go to dinner and the movies with me sometime?"

"I'd like that."

"Yay," Zoe exclaimed. "Santa made both my wishes come true."

Julie chuckled, but her heart sang with delight as she returned Dan's smile. *A date with Dan. That's the only Christmas present I need.*

A PERFECT CHRISTMAS

BY SHARON SILVA

THE SNOW BEGAN to fall around ten that morning, starting as light fluffy flakes that danced in wispy swirls on a chilly breeze—pretty, picturesque, and wrapping the town of Dogwood in a winter blanket reminiscent of a Norman Rockwell painting. Christmas lights adorned the houses and store windows, twinkling in the sparkling crystals of snow like tiny colored stars. Lighted and decorated evergreen boughs adorned the light poles along Main Street while the falling snow transformed it into the perfect winter wonderland.

It was Christmas Eve, and Lacy Morgan was in town to do some last-minute Christmas shopping. She checked her list. She'd found some fun stocking stuffers for the men at the ranch, and dog bones for the ranch's canine crew—Willow and Tucker, the two bossy Aussies that kept an eye on all of the two-legged and four-legged occupants on the property. Only the last item on her list remained—carrots and apples for the horses.

She stomped the snow from her boots at the entrance to the market and stuffed a twenty-dollar bill into the red metal bucket manned by an extremely thin Santa, who wagged an off-key gold bell. He smiled kindly and thanked her for her donation.

"Merry Christmas," she said.

"He could use a Christmas cookie or two," Chaney Roberts said softly in her ear as he walked up behind her. Snowflakes still clung to the cowboy hat that covered his jet-black hair. Chaney had some shopping of his own to do, so they'd made the trip into Dogwood together, but had gone their separate ways earlier.

"Shh," she said, holding back a laugh until they were out of earshot. "It's the Christmas season. You're supposed to be kind. Maybe he's been dieting so he can fit down all of those chimneys."

Chaney grabbed her hand then tucked it around his elbow as they walked down the produce aisle. "Well, if that's the case, you should show your Christmas spirit and buy him a pillow to tuck under his shirt. Then people like me won't come by and make comments."

"You're so bad," she chided him playfully.

"I know. And you love it." He tweaked her nose and reached for a plastic bag as she laughed out loud and gathered apples from the large wooden bin.

He was right about one thing. She definitely loved him, and loved the fact that he was with her for Christmas this year.

"Did you get your shopping done?" she asked, as she perused the apple bin, looking for the largest red apples. It was Christmas, and, this year, even the horses were going to have nothing but the best. This year, everything was going to be perfect.

He winked at her and patted his coat pocket. "Sure did. And I've got it hidden right here."

"And you're clearly not going to tell me where you went or what you bought, huh?"

"Nope. That would spoil the surprise."

"But, it is technically Christmas...Eve. Isn't that close enough?" she teased.

"No way. You have to wait until Christmas morning, or Santa will pass you right by. That's what I've been told."

She twisted her mouth and squinted at him. "Have you ever tried that out to see if it's true?'

"Nope. I'd never risk being on Santa's naughty list. But why do I have a feeling you've tried it at least once?" He gave her a phony frown from the other side of the wooden produce bin.

"Well, maybe once...."

"And how'd that work out for you?"

"It spoiled my surprise on Christmas morning." She faked a pouty face and stuck out her tongue.

"See. That wasn't just a fairy tale. It's really true." He shook his finger at her. She loved their playful banter and the twinkle in his blue eyes when he teased her. It had taken eight long years for Chaney to return to Dogwood, and now her only Christmas wish was that he would stay forever.

They both laughed as he tied up the bag of apples. "How many?" he asked, looking at the bulging bag.

"An even dozen," she said. "One for every horse."

"But we only have eleven," he said, giving her an amused smile and tilting his head.

"One for good measure." She grinned.

"That's a Morgan woman for you. Always have extra in case company shows up."

She shrugged, but turned her head to conceal her chuckle. It was in her genes. And there was more truth in what he was saying than he knew.

After selecting a dozen of the biggest carrots she could

find, they made their way to the front of the store. Chaney ribbed her about going to housewares to find a pillow for Santa's belly, while lots of people in the store smiled and wished them a Merry Christmas.

The people in Dogwood who knew Lacy and Chaney's history seemed happy to see them together, and always made a point of saying hello. Chaney no longer avoided going into town, and held his head high when he walked down the street. Dogwood was his hometown, and he had found happiness and pride in being here again.

With her grandfather's death, and myriad financial issues for the ranch, it had been a very difficult year. But so many good things had come to pass, too. With the discovery of her grandfather's will, her dream of turning the ranch into a refuge for wild and abused horses was finally becoming a reality. And Chaney was back—and they were growing closer every day. Did she dare let herself think about forever?

It was just before noon as they left the market and headed back down the street toward Chaney's truck. The snow had begun to fall heavily, and, instead of the crystal powder that had dusted the cars and the streets earlier, giant snowflakes that looked like large chunks of tissue paper now fell from the sky.

Chaney looked up at the gray clouds. "Glad we're heading home," he said. "The weather's changing fast."

He opened the door and helped her in, tucking the bags from the market around her feet, then brushed the snow from the truck windows. Her other shopping bags were neatly placed on the center of the truck seat, safely packed for the trip home. She looked over at Chaney as he climbed behind the steering wheel. Her heart warmed. He was thoughtful in so many ways.

She glanced down at the bags he'd placed so carefully. "You didn't peek, did you?" she teased.

"Only once." He shot her a mischievous look and started the truck.

"Good. There's nothing in there for you anyway. As a matter of fact, your Christmas gift hasn't been delivered yet." She gave him a smug smile and directed her gaze through the windshield.

"Ooh. Delivered. Sounds intriguing," he joked as he navigated the trusty old pickup truck out onto the street.

The wipers slapped noisily as Chaney turned them on high to keep up with the huge snowflakes that peppered down, making it difficult to see the street. Once they reached the highway and turned in the direction of the ranch, Lacy was grateful to see a snowplow up ahead. The weather always seemed to be more severe around the ranch than in town, but the property was also located closer to the mountain peaks to the west. The snow was sticking, and she was happy they only had a short distance to go. She wasn't particularly in a hurry, but she had several last-minute holiday things to take care of, and food to prepare for tonight's Christmas Eve celebration.

As the snow came down harder, a bit of worry tugged at the back of her mind. There were two very special Christmas gifts that were set to arrive at the ranch by tonight, and she hoped this storm wasn't going to interfere with either one of them.

❈ ❈ ❈

CHANEY PULLED the pickup truck into the driveway that lay between the rustic old barn and the ranch house. The snow was coming down thick and heavy. But all was good. They were home with the last-minute items, and it was definitely going to be a white Christmas. He hadn't seen one since the last time he'd spent Christmas in Dogwood, too many years ago.

The big flakes looked almost like icy white feathers falling from the sky. They melted on his face and slid down onto his collar as he came around and opened the passenger door. He sent Lacy on ahead while he gathered the bags from the truck and followed her into the house.

Walking behind her, he admired her long chestnut hair and the view of her form-fitting jeans. That was a view he'd never tire of. Seeming to sense he was watching her, she jerked her head around and shot him a wink. Apparently, she hadn't grown tired of his admiring looks, either.

Stomping the snow from their boots, they set the bags on the bench by the door and removed their heavy coats. The warmth from the old wood cookstove in the kitchen wrapped around them as they moved near it to warm their hands in its comforting glow.

Chaney pulled Lacy close and kissed the tip of her nose. "Cold as an icicle. And you were only out there a few minutes."

"I know. The temperature has really dropped since we left." She looked up at him with a twinkle in her green eyes, clearly not thinking about the weather at the moment.

He bent forward and kissed her again, lingering there and enjoying the sweet taste of her lips. Holding Lacy in his arms was the best possible gift he could receive this Christmas. In the last few months, she'd become the only thing truly important in his life.

A cold blast of air, peppered with white fluffy flakes and the sound of voices, burst through the back door at that moment as Wayne, Travis, and Brent—the ranch's foreman and his men—came into the house.

Lacy smiled, and stepped from Chaney's embrace as she greeted them. "Thanks for stoking the fire. The heat really feels good. Get out of those wet coats and come get warm. I'll make some coffee and hot cocoa."

The men were already taking off their coats, hats, and gloves, and removing their snow-covered boots. Everyone but Wayne, who stood on the rug by the back door and looked across the kitchen at Chaney. Chaney saw something in Wayne's eyes that grabbed his attention, and while Lacy busied herself with making hot drinks, Chaney moved next to Wayne.

"What's up?" Chaney asked, knowing Wayne had something on his mind.

"The Appaloosa mare got out of the corral," Wayne said softly.

The news stabbed Chaney's heart. The horse was very special to him and to Lacy. They'd been through a lot together. "How long ago?'

"Not long. She was there when I first went out, but when I went back to feed her, she was gone."

Chaney glanced over at Lacy who was laughing and joking with Travis and Brent. He didn't want to have to break that news to her on Christmas Eve.

A ripple moved through Wayne's chiseled jawline. "This storm looks like it's going to be bad. I'm going to try to find her."

Chaney nodded. "If we go now, we may be able to follow her tracks before the snow covers them over completely."

"I'm thinking the same thing." Wayne put his hand on the doorknob, and Chaney bundled up in his jacket.

"Where are you two going?" Lacy asked, a deep furrow suddenly appearing in her brow.

"To check on the livestock," Chaney said. He wasn't lying to her—he just wasn't going to be specific, and he wasn't going to tell her the mare was gone. Not yet.

He shot a glance at Travis. "Hey, can we borrow your Jeep?"

"Sure." Travis fished the keys from the pocket of his jeans and tossed them across the kitchen to Chaney.

"The cows?" she asked. "In the lower meadow?"

"We just want to be sure all the animals are safe and sound before the snow gets too bad." Chaney avoided her gaze. Looking in her eyes was risky. She could read his mind far too well.

Nothing on the ranch missed her eagle eye. This place was her dream, and she treated it with all the care and concern she possessed.

"With all the work we did to the cowsheds last fall, they should be just fine," she reminded him.

She was right. When she'd inherited the money from her grandfather's estate, she'd invested in improvements to the ranch. The cowsheds had been transformed into large, partially enclosed shelters where the cows could get in out of the weather. This storm would put those to the test, but Chaney felt sure they were going to do the job quite nicely. He nodded. "I'll feel better knowing they're all in out of the snow."

His only concern was with the mare, and time was wasting.

"Just a precaution," he said.

Travis pushed back his chair. "Want me to go with you?"

"No. You and Brent need to chop some more firewood. We may need it if the power goes out from the storm." Wayne looked over at Lacy and shot her a smile. "And one of you needs to help Lacy wrestle that big old Christmas tree out of the barn and into the house so we can decorate it later."

Travis and Brent both nodded in agreement.

"That's right," Lacy said. "So, you two don't be too long out there. It's Christmas Eve, remember?"

"We'll be back as soon as we can." Chaney followed Wayne out the back door, and Lacy gave him a scrutinizing look that told him she was suspicious.

"Good thinking with the Jeep," Wayne said, as they walked across the driveway. "I don't want to take any of the other horses out in this storm. And we'll be a darn sight warmer, too."

"Yeah. We're out to save the horse's life, not risk our own. Becoming a human popsicle isn't in my future plans."

"Nope. Mine either." The snow swirled around Wayne as he opened the door to Travis's Jeep and climbed inside. "You think she bought your story?"

"Not for a minute." But that wasn't stopping him from doing what he needed to. He had no intentions of letting anything happen to the mare or of letting it ruin Lacy's Christmas.

❧ ❧ ❧

LACY POURED CUPS of hot chocolate for Travis and Brent. She added whipped cream and peppermint candy canes to their mugs of cocoa, trying to get into the holiday spirit. She'd really been looking forward to Christmas this year, but with Chaney and Wayne going out in the storm, concern clouded her mood. There was something they weren't telling her. She could sense it.

She set the steaming cups on the table and smiled across at Travis and Brent. "Have something hot to drink, and I'll make you some sandwiches before you back out in the cold. It's well past lunchtime. You're probably both starved."

Travis smiled up at her from his seat at the table. "Thank

you, Miss Lacy. That would be great." *Yeah.* Travis was concerned about something, too. She could see it in his eyes.

"Any idea why Wayne and Chaney are worried about the livestock?"

Travis looked down at his cup of cocoa. "Just the storm, I reckon."

She turned toward the refrigerator. Full stomachs first. But Travis knew what was going on, and, clearly, he wasn't going to answer her question. Maybe she could get him to talk later.

With lunch out of the way, Lacy suggested that Travis and Brent team up on the wood, and then they would all work on the Christmas tree. Maybe Wayne and Chaney would be back by then. She should have insisted on going with them. Normally, she would have, but she needed to stay close to the house this afternoon in case Chaney's Christmas gift arrived. And she was expecting a call about another surprise as well.

She watched Brent and Travis bundle up in their heavy coats again. Her excitement rose. She couldn't wait until she could give them all their presents. This was going to be a very special holiday for everyone.

CHANEY STOPPED at the barn to get a rope, and threw a shovel in for good measure, in case they got stuck in a snowdrift. Then he and Wayne walked over to the corral to examine the mare's tracks in the snow. "She appears to be headed toward the lower pasture."

"That makes sense. That's where she and the other horses were until last week." Wayne brushed the snow from the brim of his hat, and smiled. "And we didn't lie about where we were headed."

Chaney nodded. That was good. They'd just left out a few

details—he was okay with that. He pointed at the trail of hoofprints the blowing snow was quickly covering over. "Looks like she headed toward the road a little farther down."

"Well, that was thoughtful of her, anyway," Wayne quipped, as he turned toward the Jeep.

Chaney climbed behind the wheel again and drove back onto the road.

The snow was getting deeper, but little mounds remained around the divots where the mare's hooves had plowed through the slush earlier. He was grateful for that. At least her trail was pretty easy to see from the vehicle. He shivered. At the rate the temperature was dropping, it soon wouldn't be fit out here for man or beast.

They followed the hoofmarks until they left the road, then Chaney climbed from the Jeep and called out several times. It was a longshot. The mare had been abused before Lacy took her in and cared for her, and still didn't trust humans. He couldn't blame her for that. He could only hope the sound of his voice might coax her to come to him.

Over the first few months, they'd made a lot of progress with her, and she'd gentled considerably. Chaney especially, had managed to win the mare's trust, and he was more than a little baffled at why she had run away...other than she was still wild, and obviously unpredictable.

Now he regretted that he'd put off naming the horse. But he just couldn't seem to find a name that fit.

Lacy had taken in six more wild horses last summer—rescues whose lives literally depended on finding a safe refuge. Chaney and Lacy had made the decision to let them run free in the meadow for the past few months. But the two of them had continued to interact with the horses frequently, to maintain their efforts to socialize them.

Trying to keep them contained in the corrals all the time broke Lacy's heart. They were wild creatures, and she maintained that their free spirits needed nourishing as much as their bodies. Maybe that was why the mare took off.

Chaney called several more times, but there was no sign of her. The blinding snow kept him from seeing any distance ahead of him, and the white and gray Appaloosa was going to be tough to spot in a blizzard. All they had to depend on were those small mounds of snow that marked her path through the meadow. The cold wind drove him back to the Jeep, and they continued on, following the tracks.

Wayne had been fairly quiet. "She seems to be headed toward the timber. That doesn't make a lot of sense unless she's looking for shelter." He rolled his eyes. "She had that back at the barn."

"She acted a little strange yesterday, but I didn't think too much about it."

"You think she might be sick?" Wayne asked.

Chaney was getting more concerned by the minute. "I don't know. Something just didn't seem right. All the more reason we need to find her."

LACY PULLED the last batch of gingerbread men from the oven and set the baking sheet on the counter. She took a long whiff of the spicy aroma, and her mind wandered back to her childhood, when she and her grandmother had baked Christmas cookies in the big warm kitchen while the snow pattered against the windows and the wind howled outside. There had been other Christmas Eves and other snowstorms, but none quite like this one.

Her thoughts repeatedly went to Chaney. And her mind this year wasn't just filled with Christmas past, but of Christmas future when all the love that once filled the walls of this old ranch house would live here again.

She hoped that would start with her and Chaney. With little ones of their own to share the wonderful smells, the warm cozy nights by the fireplace, and the memories as their love built a family of their own. This old ranch meant everything to her. And her dreams included making this house a home for the generations of Morgans yet to come. Did Chaney feel the same?

Brent came through the back door with an armful of firewood, pulling her from her thoughts. He and Travis now had a large pile of split logs next to the fireplace, and the wood box on the back porch was overflowing.

"It sure smells good in here," Brent said as he came back through the kitchen after depositing his load by the old rock fireplace. Leaving her cookies on the counter to cool, she pulled her coat from the hook by the door and wrapped a warm knit scarf around her neck, covering all the way to her chin.

"How about we call it good on the wood chopping and get the Christmas tree out of the barn?" she said. "Come on. It's Christmas. Let's make this old house look like it."

"That sounds great." Brent grinned, though she felt as if his mood was a little dampened. She was just grateful that he was back on his feet after he'd suffered several months with a back injury. She suspected the shadow behind his smile was because he hadn't been able to go home for Christmas this year. He'd put up a strong argument that he'd missed so much work that he just didn't feel right about being gone. Finally, she'd conceded and let him stay. But she was working on another solution to the problem, provided the storm didn't mess that up.

As the snow and cold hit her, it took her breath away. "Wow. It just keeps getting worse," she said to Brent over the howl of the wind.

She fought the knot in the pit of her stomach as she

thought of Wayne and Chaney out in the blizzard. They should be back any time. She had to have faith. They knew how to handle themselves in any kind of weather. They would be okay. Still, a prayer or two wouldn't hurt....

CHANEY NAVIGATED THE ROUGH TERRAIN. "Glad we've got a four-wheel drive."

Wayne made a clicking noise with his mouth. "Me, too. My pickup truck wouldn't have done this well in the snow. We'd have been up a creek—make that snowbank."

Chaney forced a smile. They were both getting tense as the Jeep bucked across the snow that drifted in the meadow. If the wind kept up, they would soon lose the trail. So far, it was still distinguishable.

They continued on without saying anything more. Wayne finally broke the silence. "So, did you get Lacy something special for Christmas?"

"Yeah. I did. At least, I hope she's happy with it." Chaney felt the heat come to his cheeks. He had something very special in mind, but he couldn't share his secret with Wayne. Not yet.

"She deserves it. She's had a tough year." Wayne's keen brown eyes kept watch out the passenger window while he talked.

"I know." Chaney was painfully aware of what Lacy had been through and how much she'd relied on Wayne after her grandfather passed away. "But she seems pretty happy lately."

"You've made a big difference in her, Chaney."

"Me? You think so?" Was Wayne right? Chaney hoped he was making things better at the ranch—and for her.

"I know so. You're what was missing in her life. Take it from me. I've known her a long time."

Just hearing that warmed Chaney's heart, despite the icy battle raging outside. "Thanks for telling me. It makes me feel a whole lot better."

Wayne snorted, then chuckled. "If you two don't beat all."

"What's that supposed to mean?" Chaney asked, trying not to be offended.

"I can't figure you out. You're crazy in love with each other."

"Well, yeah." The heat in his face went up several degrees. "I guess it's obvious."

Wayne shot him a look. "Well? When are you going to make this thing permanent?"

Chaney shifted in his seat. "I've thought about it." He put his hand on his coat pocket. He'd nearly forgotten that Lacy's present was still there. *Thank God I didn't lose it.*

"I'm just going to warn you. I had a woman once that I loved more than life itself." Wayne's tone had changed noticeably.

"You? I never knew that."

"I know you didn't." Wayne turned his head so he was no longer looking at Chaney. "I made the mistake of waiting too long to let her know how I felt."

"Wow. That was a lousy break."

"Yes, it was. She married someone else, and I lost her. It's been over twenty years now. Don't let that happen to you and Lacy." Wayne cleared his throat. "I'm telling you this for your own good."

Chaney thought about Wayne's words for a while. "Who was she? Someone from Dogwood?"

"Yeah. Someone who lived in Dogwood—a long time ago."

"You waited too long, huh? Why didn't you just tell her how you felt?" Chaney asked.

"Things were complicated." Wayne paused. He rubbed his hand across his chin. "She had a son."

"Oh. I see why that could have been a problem." A child could complicate things.

"He wasn't the problem. He was a really good kid." Wayne's voice faltered a bit. "I just didn't understand what she really wanted and needed from me."

"I'm sorry, Wayne. You must have really cared about her." That was becoming evident as the conversation continued. Odd that Wayne had never mentioned her before.

"I did. And I don't want to see you make the same mistake. If you really love Lacy, grab onto her and never let go."

"Sounds like great advice. I'll sure think about what you said." Chaney hesitated. He couldn't share his thoughts with Wayne, but he was glad that Wayne had shared his story.

They drove on through the howling wind and snow, searching in all directions for any sign of the mare. Chaney stopped. They'd reached the edge of the meadow where the tracks went into the trees. He glanced over at Wayne, who whistled through his teeth.

There was no driving from here. The trees were too close together, and there was too much debris on the forest floor. If they were going to find the mare, they had to go on foot from here.

LACY PUT the big box of Christmas decorations on the floor next to the tree. Travis and Brent had gone to get a ladder from the barn. After cutting away a piece of the trunk, they'd finally managed to get the spruce leveled in the tree stand without it tilting to one side or the other. That, in itself, was an accomplishment.

In the past, she'd always had an expert helper around, like her grandfather or Wayne, to help with that task. That wasn't the case today. Brent and Travis were very helpful, but their inexperience was sometimes apparent. She smiled. In a few years, they'd probably be experts at this too.

Her thoughts kept wandering to Wayne and Chaney. They'd been gone a lot longer than she had expected. She glanced again at the clock on the mantel. Over two hours had passed since they left. She tried to choke back her concern.

And then there was the matter of Chaney's Christmas gift that still hadn't arrived. She still hadn't received the promised phone call from the deliveryman, and it was almost three o'clock. Taking a deep breath, she told herself that she just had to have faith. Everything was going to work out. Unfortunately, there wasn't a darn thing she could do about the weather, and that was likely the reason for nearly everything nagging at her mind.

"I think this one will be tall enough." Travis came into the living room with the ladder, Brent right behind him.

"Looks perfect." Lacy helped him put it up next to the tree.

Brent went to work immediately, getting the lights out of the box and checking to see if they worked. Travis climbed the ladder, and Brent handed him the first string.

Well. There's a miracle in itself. No burned-out bulbs on the first strand. I hope it's a good omen.

She held onto the ladder, making sure it didn't tip while Travis reached up to string the lights. "Too bad Chaney and Wayne aren't back yet. They're going to miss all of the fun."

"Yeah. I'd hoped they'd be back by now." Travis worked extra hard to get the light at the treetop to stand straight.

"Wish I knew what was going on with them," Lacy hinted. "Then maybe I wouldn't be so worried that they aren't back yet."

Travis glanced down at her, a small furrow in his brow. "Don't worry, Miss Lacy. They'll probably be back any time."

"I just hope they're okay."

Brent was preoccupied with changing bulbs in a string of lights, but chimed in too. "I'm sure if they'd found the horse, they'd be back by now."

Travis's head spun toward Brent, and he shot daggers with his eyes.

The ladder rocked. Lacy instinctively steadied it before she reacted to Brent's comment. "What horse?"

"Brent, doggone it," Travis grumbled. He looked down at Lacy. "We weren't supposed to say anything." Travis hung the string of lights on the top rung and backed down the ladder.

Brent looked at Travis and shrugged. "I'm sorry. I wasn't thinking, and it just slipped out."

Lacy nailed Travis with her eyes. "I knew you were covering for them. Come on, spill it. What horse? What's going on?"

Travis took a deep breath and looked down at his boots. "The Appaloosa. She got out of the corral."

Her heart sank. "What? How did she get out?" No wonder Chaney had gone after her in spite of the storm. They both had so much of themselves invested in that horse.

"We don't know. She was gone when Wayne went to feed her." Brent looked like he felt sick. She wasn't sure if that was because the horse was gone, or because he'd spilled the beans.

"They're trying to follow her tracks, I suppose," Travis put in. "Wayne was real upset about it."

Her gut knotted. Her first instinct was to go after them, to try to find Wayne and Chaney. But that sure wasn't going to help the situation. In this storm, it would be next to impossible. Not to mention, Travis and Brent would never let her go alone. Then they'd all be out there in danger, and something bad was bound to happen. *Well, shoot. All I can do is wait.*

"This storm is really getting bad." Brent said. "I hope they're okay."

"Well, one thing's for sure." She looked from Travis to Brent and then back again, trying to calm the storm brewing within her. "At least now I know *why* I should be worried."

CHANEY FOLLOWED Wayne through the pine trees, not surprised that he'd insisted on leading the way. Their scarves were wrapped around their heads and covered their faces, leaving only a small gap for their eyes, as they tried to avoid frostbite from the nipping wind and cold. Maybe he should have asked Santa for a ski mask for Christmas.

Chaney carried a rope in one gloved hand, and he'd left Lacy's gift in the glove box of the Jeep this time, not wanting to risk it falling out of his pocket. They walked on for at least a half mile, tripping now and then on fallen limbs hidden by the snow, and avoiding bulging tree roots that were covered by slippery tree needles on the forest floor.

"See anything?" Chaney yelled to Wayne. Snow was sticking in his eyelashes so badly, he was having a hard time seeing what was ahead.

"Just a few more tracks. No other sign of her."

"How far to the fence line?" Chaney asked.

"At least another half mile."

Chaney nodded, though it was doubtful Wayne could see it the way he was bundled up. "You okay?"

"Cold, but hanging in," Wayne yelled over the howling wind. Wayne was nearly covered in white as the snow blew into his face. He resembled a snowman, but it was hard to find humor in that under the circumstances. Chaney was pretty sure he looked the same way.

"Let's try to get to the fence," Chaney said. Fear tugged at the back of his mind. If they didn't find the mare soon, they'd have to give up. It was getting riskier to be out in this storm. And how long would it be before they wouldn't be able to get back to the house?

They trudged on a little farther. Wayne stopped and looked around. "I think we've lost her trail."

Chaney scanned the area, trying to identify the variances in the snow that could possibly be her tracks. It was getting harder here in the forest with the undulations in the terrain and limbs scattered under the snow.

His heart sank. He walked in a circle around a big pine tree, trying to see any identifying marks. Wayne walked with him, helping him look. Chaney ducked under a low tree branch and, as he came back up, his eye caught something moving up ahead. "Wayne. I think I see something."

"Where?"

Chaney put his hand on Wayne's shoulder and pointed up ahead of them and to the right. The large white blur moved again. They walked toward it.

When they were a dozen or more yards away, they saw the faint outline of a horse huddled beneath the drooping limbs of a pine tree. The animal moved, shaking the snow from its coat. Chaney got a glimpse of the gray and white spots on the mare's rump.

"It's her." Chaney lowered his voice, fearing the horse would spook. He stepped around Wayne. "Wait here."

Wayne moved a little closer to the base of a nearby tree, either trying to blend in, or trying to use its branches as shelter.

Chaney took slow, careful steps. The mare saw him. She raised her head and nickered softly.

"That's right, girl. It's me."

The horse shook again, sending clumps of melting snow flying. She moved closer to the tree trunk. Ever since Chaney had come to the ranch, he'd had a special bond with the mare. Under his breath, he prayed that she'd remember that and not try to run away.

He slowly raised the rope. She watched him intently, snorting and throwing her head back. Maybe that was a bad idea. He lowered the rope again. He had no idea what the mare had been through with her previous owner, but she'd been abused. He had to try to anticipate anything that might frighten her. Throwing a lasso around her neck might not be a good idea. He moved a few steps closer. She remained still.

It took several minutes of walking slowly to get close enough for her to extend her muzzle toward him.

"That's right. It's okay, girl." The howling storm prevented her from hearing his words.

He edged closer, hoping she would stay put. Finally, within earshot, he realized he was probably going to have to use his old reliable method of calming her down. He began to hum, then sing. Forced to raise his voice above normal, he feared he might frighten her, but she just twitched her ears and listened intently.

He sang her the song that he'd used when he had calmed her the very first time. After a few choruses, he shifted to the words of his favorite carol, "Silent Night, Holy Night." The song he'd sung in church on Christmas Eve when he was a boy. It conjured memories of him standing next to his mother, his hand pressed in hers.

The mare seemed to like it. And it warmed his insides as well. Anything to keep them both focused.

Within a few minutes, the horse let him approach. He placed his cheek against her jaw, and she leaned into him. Then he carefully tied the rope to her halter. He kept singing as he led her back toward Wayne, who had been watching and waiting under the tree. Wayne turned and led the way back through the forest, following their rapidly disappearing tracks back to the Jeep.

Once they got to the vehicle, Wayne quickly cleared the windows. Chaney continued his singing. He stopped for just a second to speak. "You drive. I'm going to hang out the window and lead her back."

Wayne waved to him, careful not to startle the mare, and climbed into the driver's seat. Chaney rolled down the passenger window and maneuvered inside, keeping the rope in his hand, never missing a chorus of the carol.

The mare seemed startled when the Jeep started up, but Chaney was ready for that and kept his face close to her head so she could hear his voice above the engine and the storm. Slowly, Wayne drove the Jeep back through the drifted pasture. They both breathed a sigh of relief when they turned back onto the road.

Chaney glanced over at Wayne who was defrosting a little, and changed his Christmas song over to "Frosty the Snowman."

Wayne took note. "Yeah, and you're gonna look like Rudolph by the time we get to the house with your head hanging out the window."

Chaney laughed. He couldn't respond with a wisecrack without stopping his singing, but he sure had a lot of them running through his head. Wayne's jovial spirit had returned. He'd been so serious earlier when he talked about losing the woman he loved. Wayne's heart had once been broken. The story made Chaney look at Wayne differently. He'd always thought of him as a loner. Now he knew that wasn't the case.

Chaney pulled his thoughts back to the mare and his song. As long as she could hear Chaney's voice, the mare stayed close to the vehicle and walked along. When he stopped, she pulled away and fought the rope. So, despite his now-scratchy throat, he sang.

He was happy despite the conditions as they drove back slowly through the blizzard. It was getting dark now, and it was going to take a while to walk the mare back to the house, but it was going to be okay. He and Wayne had saved Christmas for Lacy. They were bringing the mare home.

FROST CRYSTALS FORMED in the corners of the kitchen window as Lacy watched for any sign of headlights in the blustering storm. She warmed her hands on the hot coffee mug she held and let out a long sigh. It was dark now. Even though it was December and darkness came before five o'clock, that was little consolation. Chaney and Wayne had been gone for hours. Chaney's cell phone lay on the counter, taunting her. Why hadn't he taken it with him? If he had, at least she would know if he was safe.

Her hopes of a perfect Christmas were crumbling fast. The two people she cared about most in the world were out there, somewhere in this awful blizzard. Brent and Travis were now out doing evening chores, and she had lost interest in trimming the tree. Even the distraction of trying over and over to reach the phone number to inquire about Chaney's present only took her mind away from her worries for a little while. And she knew the answer to that question already. The delivery wasn't going to happen because of the storm.

The same with Brent's gift. His was on an airplane flying into DIA and then being delivered from there. The evening news blared on about all of the flight cancellations and the traffic snarls. *Nope.* That wasn't happening either.

Under normal circumstances, all of that would have upset her, but all she wanted was for everyone to get back to the house safe and sound tonight. The rest of it didn't seem that important.

This was her first Christmas with Chaney in such a long time, and she wanted it to be perfect. And up until a few hours ago, it had been. Now she tried to calm her fears that a tragedy might ruin everything.

Please, Lord, just bring them back safe. She stopped before she went on. It was almost too much to ask that they'd find the mare in this blizzard, too.

Her heart broke, thinking of the mare wandering in this storm. But maybe the horse had good instincts. She'd survived an abusive owner and overcome the odds by surviving her infected wounds during last summer's floods. She was a survivor. And so was Lacy. But she still couldn't understand what would have possessed the animal to run away in the middle of a snowstorm.

Brent and Travis came through the back door, stomping the snow from their boots.

"Brr. That wind is fierce," Travis said, then glanced at her as if he'd said something wrong. He was always very kind, and she was sure he didn't want to add to her concern.

She tried to force a smile. "Yes. You'd better call it good for tonight."

The smell of the turkey roasting in the oven filled the kitchen, but even that didn't bring the normal enthusiasm from either of them. It was clear that worry was dampening everyone's holiday mood.

Willow and Tucker lay under the kitchen table. Even they hadn't shown an interest in going along to do the chores. That was highly unusual. Lacy suspected the dogs were just picking up on everyone else's worry.

Travis and Brent had taken off their coats and boots and were now sitting at the kitchen table, looking glum. She blew out a long breath. "Let's work on the tree. It'll give us something to keep our minds occupied."

Pouring her now-cold coffee down the kitchen sink, she took one last glance out the window. *Wait. Are those headlights?* She stopped and leaned closer. *Yes.* Travis's jeep eased into the driveway.

"They're back," she shouted, running toward the door, followed by Travis, Brent, Tucker, and Willow. While the humans struggled with their coats and boots, Willow stood at the back door and barked several times. Tucker whirled around in a happy dance behind her.

Lacy was the first one out, still struggling with her coat buttons, and her scarf trailed over her shoulder. Tucker was close at her heels. Joy shot through her, but she slowed a little as she saw Chaney walking the mare toward the barn. Tucker followed suit. She struggled to contain herself. Chaney was home, and he'd found the horse, too. She wanted more than anything to run and throw her arms around him, but wouldn't risk spooking the mare.

The faint strains of a Christmas carol filled the air as they walked away. Leave it to Chaney. He had a way with that horse, and the mare couldn't resist him when he sang to her. *Thank you, God, for giving Chaney that gift.*

She stopped long enough to hug Wayne, who was out of the Jeep and having an animated conversation with Travis and Brent. Lacy only heard bits of it, but it didn't matter. They were safe. They were *all* safe.

Willow couldn't restrain herself any longer and tackled Tucker, who was wagging his stubby tail and wiggling all over in anticipation. The two rolled through the snow, barking and giving each other love nips. Lacy smiled—she was going to follow Willow's lead. She headed toward the barn to find Chaney. She was going to squeeze the stuffing out of him.

She cautiously entered the barn, making sure Chaney had the mare secured in a stall. He had latched the gate of the enclosure, and was removing the rope as she walked up behind him.

He turned and she grabbed him around the waist and squeezed his as tight as she could. "Chaney Roberts, don't you ever scare me like that again," she blurted. "I was so worried."

He spun and threw his arms around her, hugging her back as tightly as she was holding him. She looked up and his lips met hers, kissing her long and deep. "I'm sorry. I just didn't want you to lose your mare on Christmas. I had to find her."

"I know what you did." She stared up into his eyes. "You were trying to protect me, as always. You are such an amazing man, but really—"

He cut off her words with another kiss, then finished her sentence for her. "—but really, it's Christmas Eve, and we have a lot to celebrate. First, I'm going to take care of the mare, then we're going to get on with the holiday."

He put down the rope as she reached and put her hand on top of his. "No. *We're* going to take care of the mare and then *we're* going to celebrate. We've got a tree to trim and the turkey is in the oven."

"Great. I can't wait to try out the mistletoe." he said, slapping her gently on the hip.

She giggled. "Got that covered, too."

CHANEY GRABBED a brush from a nearby stall and, after he spoke softly and moved slowly, the mare allowed him to remove most of the snow from her coat.

"I'm not sure why she tried to run away," he said. "Maybe

I should have put her in the barn with Inca and Cricket earlier."

"This wasn't your fault. I didn't want to put her into the big corral with the wild horses. And she's always been restless in tight places. She's *seemed* content in the small corral."

Chaney shook his head. "She's different from the wild ones. She's been trained. It's just that the abuse she went through did a number on her. But she's come a long way since you brought her here."

"I know. It's amazing how she filled out so fast after being half-starved."

"She sure has." Chaney had a hunch what was going on with the horse, but he wasn't going to say anything. "You got her in early May, right?"

"That's right. The week before you came back to Dogwood."

Chaney nodded. Then he gathered some old towels and a stable blanket from the next stall. It was evident that the mare was cold, and the melting snow and moisture in her coat wasn't helping. She stood still and allowed Chaney to dry her back and the sides of her belly with the towels before he reached over the stall and carefully eased the blanket onto her back. She flinched a little at first, but soon seemed to appreciate its warmth.

Lacy had a bucket of oats and, for the first time, the mare didn't shy away when Lacy approached. Lacy hung the bucket on a post and the mare ate hungrily.

Lacy smiled. "These are her favorite. The ones with molasses."

Chaney looked over at Lacy. His heart warmed at how she was always thinking of the best interests of everyone and everything on the ranch. She was nothing short of amazing—only one of the reasons why he loved her so much.

"Well, I think she's settled in. How about we get to the house and get ourselves warm?"

Lacy's eyes sparkled as she looked over at him. "Thank you, Chaney. If it weren't for you, she'd be out in the storm, and who knows what would have happened to her."

Chaney shrugged. "I have to take care of my girls." And that's exactly what he planned to keep doing.

LACY SERVED up a turkey dinner with all the trimmings that everyone seemed to enjoy. Spirits had lifted, and the men laughed and joked over big slices of pumpkin pie and coffee. Lacy slipped away a few times to call the phone number again, hoping beyond hope that Chaney's gift would still make it.

The last time she dialed, instead of a busy signal, she got a recording saying the company was closed for the holidays. Disappointment flooded through her, but she recovered quickly. She had to keep things in perspective. They were all safe and warm. And they were all going to be together for Christmas.

She made a quick check on her phone, and was dizzied by the number of airline flights that were cancelled. That only confirmed that she wouldn't have a surprise for Brent, either. The storm had wreaked havoc on her gift-giving efforts, but she wouldn't let it ruin their Christmas.

After dinner, they all tackled the bare Christmas tree and the box of decorations. It wasn't long before the twinkling tree lights and the pungent smell of evergreen filled the living room with the glorious sights and smells of Christmas.

Wayne built a fire in the fireplace while they all scurried off to their respective rooms and returned with arms filled with gifts to put underneath the tree. Lacy brought out what she had, still feeling bad about the two missing gifts, but resolved to make the best of it.

They sat by the fire and shared eggnog and stories they remembered from their childhoods, each of them sharing the story of their favorite Christmas. Lacy and Chaney snuggled close on the sofa, both saying that this was their favorite Christmas so far.

Wayne was quiet and seemed to want to keep his favorite Christmas to himself, saying only that it was the one he'd shared with a very special lady.

Travis said he'd had so many when he was growing up that it would be hard to choose just one. His parents had gone out of state this year, and it was the first time he hadn't been with them.

Brent started to tell about his, but seemed a little misty-eyed as he talked of his mother. Brent was barely twenty, but seemed a lot older than his years. He stopped halfway through and couldn't go on. Lacy's heart clenched in her chest. That only made her feel worse that she wasn't going to be able to give him the gift she'd planned.

The group laughed and talked and stayed up way past their bedtime, as was the usual rule in the Morgan house on Christmas Eve. Lacy's grandparents had always been up until after midnight as a family tradition on the holiday. Her grandmother always said that she waited all year for Christmas, and she wasn't going to waste any of it sleeping. And so, the Christmas Eve family tradition was born, along with the turkey dinners and the eggnog, and the whole family trimming the tree. And, the following day, they'd get up and start celebrating all over again.

Just before midnight, Wayne said he was going to go out and check on the mare and ensure the barn was secure. "I don't have another outing like the one we had today left in me," he said to Chaney. "I'm going to be darn sure our little escape artist is where we left her."

"I'll go with you," Chaney said, and after giving Lacy one more kiss under the mistletoe, he pulled on his coat and followed Wayne outside.

Travis yawned. "This has been one of the nicest Christmas Eves I can remember. I hate to see it end."

Lacy smiled. "Oh, we still have tomorrow. We do Christmas right at the Second Chance Ranch."

They were all laughing as the back door opened and Chaney called to them from the kitchen. "You all need to put on your coats and come out to the barn. There's something you've got to see."

"Seriously?" Lacy called back, getting up from the sofa. "It's midnight and it's still snowing. This had better be good."

Chaney was standing by the door, grinning from ear to ear. He was covered with snow that was melting onto the floor, but his eyes were shining with delight.

"What is it?" she asked, as she pulled on her boots, growing more curious by the minute.

"You'll see. Just hurry up."

"From the look on his face, he must have seen Santa Claus," Travis joked.

"Yeah. Or stepped in reindeer droppings in the driveway," Brent chimed in.

"You two pipe down. If you don't think it's worth the trip out in the cold, I'll buy the next round of eggnogs."

"Very funny," Travis mumbled through the scarf that now covered his mouth.

They all waded through the snow, single file, trying to stay in Chaney's big footsteps as he led the way to the barn. The snow was still falling, and was nearly up to their knees. A sliver of the moon peeked through the heavy clouds, lighting the yard just enough to make the snow look like a silver blanket.

"Isn't it beautiful?" Lacy said. "It looks like a Christmas card."

"Looks like a blanket to me," Travis said. "Like the one on my bed that's calling my name."

"Don't be such a whiner," Chaney said. "It's pretty evident you've already missed your beauty sleep."

"That was cold," Brent said. "Almost as cold as my toes."

They were all still ribbing each other as Chaney opened the barn door. By the dim light in the barn, they could see Wayne standing next to the stall that held the Appaloosa mare. Wayne put his fingers to his lips and signaled them to be quiet.

Chaney held the door and motioned Lacy to go inside first. The others followed. As Lacy approached the stall, Wayne looked over the rail and pointed to something on the floor inside. Lacy gasped. Nestled in the straw at the mare's feet was a tiny gray-and-white speckled colt.

"Oh my gosh." Her eyes met Chaney's. "She was pregnant?"

Chaney smiled. "Yep. She was with foal when you got her."

Lacy still couldn't get over it. "How could we have missed that?"

Wayne shrugged. "It's unusual not to be able to tell, but it happens, especially with first-timers. Lots of things fooled us. She was half-starved and slow getting up to her normal feeding habits."

"Yeah," Chaney put in. "With everything she went through, she just didn't show. She was thin for so long, and this baby isn't very big. But Wayne and I checked him out. He's strong, and seems to be a healthy little guy."

Wayne patted Lacy's shoulder. "Don't you worry too

much. We'll watch him real close and we'll have Dr. Donovan check him out just as soon as she can."

It was hard to tell which one of them was prouder of the colt. Chaney was still smiling. "I was suspicious when we brought her back today, but I didn't want to say anything. That's why she ran away. She was looking for a place in the woods to have her baby."

"Why would she do that?" Brent asked, looking at the tiny horse in wonder.

"Just following her instincts," Chaney said.

Brent was still amazed. "Even in a blizzard?"

"I suspect that she was a wild horse at one time. That explains why she is so afraid of people," Chaney went on.

"I think you're right. Whoever bought her may not have known, and when he couldn't handle her, he tried to beat her into submission," Wayne put in. "Sad for her, but probably what happened."

Lacy was sure of one thing. "Well, she's found her forever home now. And no one will ever treat her or her baby badly."

Chaney put an arm around Lacy's waist and pulled her to him. "Merry Christmas. You just got the first foal to be born on the Second Chance Ranch for a present."

Lacy glanced over at Wayne who wore a wide smile. "The first of many, Miss Lacy." She detected a little moisture in the corner of his eye.

Lacy brushed away a tear of her own and knelt down, putting her hand through the slats on the stall and touching the baby's nose. "I'm going to name you Miracle. Because you're just one of the many miracles that have come into my life this year and made my dreams come true."

Chaney put his hand on her back. "Guess we should come up with a name for her mama, too."

"I'm going to leave that up to you. After all, you're her favorite."

Chaney grinned. "I'd been waiting on you, but I kind of like Elsa."

"Oh, I like it. And so appropriate, too."

"Yes. And Elsa means wild at heart. It all fits her."

"Then Elsa it is. Elsa and baby Miracle."

"Well, let's go back where it's warm," Chaney said. He headed for the door and opened it wide for the others. Wayne brought up the rear, leaving the light on in the barn. Lacy knew he'd be coming back to keep an eye on the new baby.

As Lacy stepped onto the driveway, she heard a low roar and looked up the road. Headlights were coming down the road into the ranch.

"Who the heck could that be this time of the night?" Wayne asked from behind her.

"What the...?" Chaney said softly.

They all stepped to the side of the driveway and watched and waited as the headlights drew nearer and the sound of an engine grew louder. By the time it reached the gate into the ranch, Lacy could make out the outline of a big pickup truck. It appeared to be pulling a trailer.

"It can't possibly be..." she whispered.

The big pickup truck with oversized tires pulled into the driveway. Between the glare of the headlights and the falling snow, it was impossible to see the driver until he climbed out of the truck. An older man dressed in a long-sleeved red T-shirt and bright Christmas-patterned suspenders turned to look at them. Lacy's mouth dropped open as she saw his white hair and long white beard. The blue jeans and cowboy boots didn't fit the picture that conjured in her head, nor did his red baseball cap, but who was she to question such attire?

"Are you Miss Lacy Morgan?" he asked in a deep, jolly voice.

Words escaped her. Chaney put his hand on her shoulder. "This is Lacy," he answered for her.

"I have a delivery for you. Sorry to be so late, but the roads are terrible out there."

Lacy just nodded, but finally found her voice. "My delivery? Really?" She glanced back at the horse trailer, nearly as stunned by the fact that it was here as she was by the appearance of the driver.

"We promised delivery by Christmas Eve." The man looked at his watch. "I only missed it by a few minutes."

"Oh. No worries here," she stammered. Finally regaining her ability to communicate, she walked to the back of the trailer with the driver while the others looked from one to the other with questioning looks. The man lowered the ramp of the long trailer, and walked inside. She waited, excitement crawling through her with each footstep she took.

She couldn't see inside the trailer, but within a few minutes, the man came down the ramp leading a beautiful black Arabian stallion. He handed her the lead rope.

"Thank you so much," she whispered. "He's beautiful. I can't believe you got through this storm."

The man smiled and gave her a wink. "I make a special effort when it's a really important gift."

Lacy led the horse around to the front of the truck and stopped just short of where the others stood in front of the barn door.

She handed the rope to Chaney, then raised on her tip toes and kissed him. "Merry Christmas."

Chaney's expression was awestruck. "He's mine?"

"If you're going to be a permanent fixture around here, you need your own horse," she said.

She caught Wayne's grin from the corner of her eye as he did a fist pump and mouthed a thank-you up to the sky.

The driver tapped her on the shoulder. "I've just got one more thing for you, ma'am. If you could follow me..."

Lacy walked around to the other side of the truck, expecting he had some paperwork for her to sign. He opened the passenger door and assisted an older woman from the truck cab.

The woman wasn't really dressed for the snow, but had a reasonable coat on, unlike the man.

The woman beamed. "You must be Lacy. I'm Brent's mother."

Lacy could hardly believe her ears. "How the... What on earth?" She looked over at the man in the red shirt, suddenly realizing how chubby he was. Her mind whirled.

The woman leaned closer. "My plane was late getting into DIA because of the weather. The bus brought me as far as Dogwood, but somewhere along the way, I lost your phone number. I met this nice man at the coffee shop and he said he was coming out to the Morgan ranch. I hope I didn't spoil your surprise."

"Oh my gosh, no. I thought your flight had been cancelled, along with all of the others."

The man pulled a suitcase from the truck cab and held it out for the woman. Lacy took it from him and grabbed the woman's hand. They walked through the headlights and around to the group by the barn.

Brent looked over at them and blinked his eyes as if he thought he was dreaming. "Mom? Mom!"

Brent threw his arms around her and lifted her off the ground.

"Oh my," the woman said. "It's been way too long."

Lacy was bursting with joy. "All my Christmas gifts seem be arriving at once." She handed the suitcase to Brent. "Get your mom in out of the snow. Chaney, you've got a horse to bed down for the night."

As the others went on their way, she turned toward the driver and gave him a giant hug. Suddenly struck by the fact that the man was out in the snow without a coat, she asked. "Aren't you cold?"

"Nope." He chuckled. "I live where it's much colder than this."

"You're welcome to stay the night and wait for the snow to stop," she offered. "We have plenty of room."

He gave her another wink and climbed into his truck. "Oh, no. Much obliged, but I've got to be going. Lots to do. Christmas Eve, you know."

He turned the truck around in the driveway loop as she walked back to the house, and the red tail lights disappeared into the distance. If she wasn't a grownup, she could almost swear she'd just met Santa Claus.

❖ ❖ ❖ ❖

CHANEY SETTLED his beautiful stallion in a stall, and reluctantly left him to join the others in the house. After a quick stop to retrieve something from the Jeep, he opened up the back door to the sounds of laughter. Though it was well after midnight, everyone was so excited, they wouldn't be sleeping any time soon.

Lacy greeted him at the living room door. "I'm glad you're here. Since it's officially Christmas morning, I'm not waiting to give Wayne and Travis their gifts."

She walked over and pulled a gift bag from under the tree. "Wayne," she said as she handed it to him.

Wayne smiled broadly, and pulled a sheet of paper from the bag. He looked at it, then looked up at her. "What is this?" he asked.

"The bill of sale for two registered Angus cattle." Lacy's eyes sparkled with happiness. "I'm putting you in charge of that side of the operation, and those two cows are going to belong solely to you."

"I don't know what to say." Wayne's voice wavered as he spoke.

"Don't say anything. You've earned it."

She walked over to the loveseat and stood in front of Travis. "Travis, your gift isn't wrapped. You're getting a promotion of sorts. I'm putting you in charge of acquisitions for the ranch."

He looked at her puzzled. "Ma'am?"

"Four-legged acquisitions. I want you to deal with the rescues and getting them to the ranch. In particular, the wild horses. I'll have a say, of course, but you'll be in charge of the rest."

"Why, Miss Lacy. I'm speechless. That's my dream job."

"I know. My dreams are coming true, and I want you all to see your dreams happen, too." She smiled over at Brent and his mother. They were both beaming.

Chaney stood aside, watching Lacy enjoy the happiness she had spread around the room.

The phone on Chaney's hip buzzed. "Who on earth is messaging me this time of night?" he asked out loud, looking down at his phone. "Huh. It's my mom. She says Merry Christmas to everyone. Well, I'll be darned. She's moving back to Dogwood."

Wayne grabbed his eggnog, offered a toast and downed the rest. Was Chaney imagining things, or had Wayne said "yes!" under his breath.

Lacy beamed. "That's another wonderful surprise for you, Chaney. I'm fresh out of them. Maybe we should save the rest of the gifts for in the morning."

Chaney stepped around the end of the sofa. "Not so fast. There's one more dream come true that hasn't been addressed."

Lacy looked at him curiously. "I missed something?"

"No. I did." Chaney moved his hand from behind his back and opened it, showing her the small black box. Her face paled, and she covered her mouth with her hand.

"Lacy Morgan, will you do me the honor of being my wife?" He opened the box carefully, exposing the sparkling diamond surrounded by tiny horseshoes set with sapphires.

"Oh, Chaney. There's nothing I want more." She threw her arms around his neck, and he pulled her to him. First, he kissed her lips, then the tear that slid down her cheek.

"Don't cry. This is the happiest day of my life," he said, blinking back the moisture in his own.

"I can't help it. I've never been so happy."

Chaney pulled Lacy into his arms as the others filtered out of the room, offering hugs and congratulations. Chaney looked over at Wayne, who was smiling like the cat who ate the canary.

When they were alone at last, he whispered, "Merry Christmas, sweetheart. I love you."

She leaned into his arms. "I love you, too. Thank you for making this a perfect Christmas."

Yes. It was perfect. But he'd had a little help from his friends and a lot from the man upstairs.

OPERATION: CHRISTMAS SURPRISE

BY LAURA HAYDEN

"WHAT DO you mean the deal is off?" Annemarie Handley stared at her sister, Ella, who was doing her best not to cry.

Ella swiped a sleeve across her face. "The building has been sold, and the new owner is breaking their lease in order to tear the whole thing down."

Annemarie tried not to show her relief. In her opinion, her parents had made a foolish…no, an overly generous and mostly unwise decision to back Ella's dreams to own Eats & Treats, the local bakery where she'd been working since graduating from culinary school. The building was old— and not in a historical registry sort of way, Ella was too young, and such a venture would mean taking a big hit to the Handley Retirement Fund.

Annemarie knew, because she kept the books for her family and their business. Ella might not be a spoiled brat, but she'd always had a way to convince their parents to do things that neither Annemarie nor her brother, Trey, would have ever contemplated. The two of them chalked it up to the age difference between them and Ella. Their little sister had been what her Great Aunt Marie called, an "oops" baby, born almost nine years after Annemarie.

Both Trey and Annemarie believed that those nine years had mellowed their parents. As a result, Ella had a car at sixteen—albeit a junker that she had to learn to repair—and went to three different colleges until finding her bliss outside of the traditional classroom and in the kitchen, instead.

And now, the so-called brat of the family—whom Annemarie had to admit wasn't really bratty at all—sat across the table, doing an admirable job of hiding her disappointment.

"I talked to them about just buying the equipment, but the ovens were custom built-ins, and I'd have to take them out, and put them in storage until I found a new storefront with suitable size and the right location. Then I'd have to design a kitchen to accommodate them, and then figure out how to install them. That's a lot more complicated than I need."

It was times like these that reminded her that her little sister was indeed growing up. Annemarie put on her bravest face. "We should tell Dad. Maybe he can figure something out. If anyone can, it's him."

ELLA BROKE the news to the rest of their family at dinner that night. As expected, as soon as the meal was over, their father scurried off to his office where Annemarie suspected he called the bakery's owners, Earl and May Sinclair, to learn more about this sudden reversal of plans.

Ella cornered Annemarie after he left. "Can't you stop him? The Sinclairs feel bad enough without him grilling them."

"He's not going to grill them." Her father was the soul of diplomacy, and she trusted him to broach the subject without causing friction. "He's simply going to see if there are any angles they haven't thought of, yet. You know him and his 'think outside the box' way of working through problems."

"Outside the box. Right."

Her mom dried her hands on a kitchen towel and gave them both a vanilla-scented hug. "So, while your dad is looking into this, why don't we start baking the cookies?"

Every Christmas, their mother, Lydia Handley, managed a huge Christmas Cookie Exchange. It'd become a tradition in town, and now that the town's best bakery was going to go out of business, the exchange might become even more important. So the three women piled into the kitchen and started pulling out ingredients. Although Ella was the official baking professional in the family, their mother still commanded the kitchen, making the decision on which of their exchange favorites to bake. The decision? Mrs. Claus's Buttons, which were raspberry jam-filled sugar cookies, and Pistachio Linzer Cookies, both of which would keep well in the freezer until closer to the event.

As she worked the dough, Annemarie turned to her sister. "So you're going to make your Dogwood Bites this year, right?"

Ella's burst of laughter both surprised and pleased Annamarie. "I will," she said, "but this year, I'll make sure the tags say something other than K-9 CHRISTMAS COOKIES. Mrs. Harrington still gives me the stink eye over that."

Her mom giggled. "I know she's allergic to dogs, but to decide it means she's also allergic to dog cookies is completely insane. She acted as if we were trying to poison her."

"But that was only after she found out they were for dogs. Before that, she was saying how good they tasted."

They continued to regale each other with cookie

exchange stories as they prepped the Buttons dough and then placed it in the fridge to chill and started on the Linzer cookies. When their mother realized she didn't have enough confectioner's sugar, Ella offered to run to the store and get more.

As soon as she'd departed, Annamarie's father stuck his head in the kitchen. "Where's Little Bit?"

"Gone to the store," her mother answered.

"Good." He took a quick look as if assuring himself that his youngest was truly gone, then turned back to them, rubbing his hands. "Trey and I have been cooking up a plan. I think I know how to help Ella realize her dream. The only thing is…she's going to have to change her dream a little."

"What do you mean, Doug?" her mom chided.

"What if I told you Old Bessy was going to ride again?"

THAT NIGHT DRIVING HOME, Annamarie mulled over her father's rather grandiose plans that they somehow managed to keep secret from the youngest in the family. Ella excelled in the art of snooping, as evidenced by the fact she knew every Christmas present weeks in advance, and always figured out where keys to important things were hidden—like diaries and keys to liquor cabinets. Keeping a secret from Ella Handley would take finesse, cunning, and a codebook committed to memory. They'd even code-named it Operation: Christmas Surprise.

And the grandiose plan?

It involved Bessy the Bus, which had been Dogwood Express's very first transportation vehicle—the reason why her parents met and eventually fell in love. The bus held a special place in all of their lives. When she was young, the bus had still made occasional runs to pick up shelter dogs and bring them to Sanctuary. When she grew older, it became her playhouse. Her father even taught her how to drive a manual by letting her grind through the gears in the school parking lot on Sundays. And although Bessy still had the ability to run—thanks to her father's handiwork—the bus was no longer capable of pulling the steep mountain roads, or doing anything beyond tooling around town at sedate speeds.

The perfect vehicle for an in-town, mobile bakery that stayed more than it moved.

Her father could get the vehicle running properly, overhaul the engine, and put on new tires, but turning it into a mobile bakery required talents and skills that none of them had. Annamarie knew who she should call for their missing expertise...

But could she?

Ella was the one who'd introduced Annamarie to Giovanni "Gio" Tanner. The two had met in culinary school and studied together, but no romantic sparks flew. "He's like a second big brother," Ella had explained.

But when Annamarie met him—fireworks!

But like most fireworks, their relationship had started with a big bang, then after that, the smoke gently floated in the sky and slowly dissipated. To this day, Annamarie wasn't sure why they broke up, but it hadn't been acrimonious or dramatic. So that's why she only hesitated for a couple of minutes before calling him.

He sounded sleepy. "Ella?"

"No, it's me, Annemarie."

"Annie!" He perked up immediately and used a nickname for her that she hated people using—except for him. "Is everything okay?"

"Oh, sure. I didn't wake you, did I?"

He chuckled. "Yeah, but when did that stop you?"

"Sorry. I'll call you back in the morning."

"No, no. How th' heck are you? We haven't talked in ages."

"I'm good."

"Your mom and dad? Trey?"

"All fine. It's Ella."

If he had been sleepy before, he sounded wide-awake now. "Is everything okay? I just talked to her a couple of weeks ago. Everything was fine then."

"Don't panic. She's fine, just heartbroken."

Gio became all business. "Tell me his name. I'll make his life miserable."

"Slow your roll, it's not a guy. It's a bakery."

"So is there a problem with the place she wants to buy?"

"'Fraid so. The deal fell through."

He went back to his male posturing. "Like I said, tell me his name. I'll make his life miserable."

"You'll do nothing of the sort," she chided him. "Mr. Sinclair and his wife are absolutely gems, and they're heartbroken, too. The landlord sold the building out from beneath them, and the new owner is breaking the lease and tearing the whole structure down."

"Tell me his—"

"Gio, will you stop playing *quien es mas macho*—or whatever the Italian equivalent of that is? I don't need your fists, I need your brain."

"I'm listening. And it's *chi ha le palle di farlo?*"

She ignored her lesson in conversational Italian. "I don't know if Ella ever mentioned Bessy the Bus to you, but Bessy is an old school bus that has a real sentimental place in our lives. My dad wants to turn it into a mobile food truck so El can have a bakery on wheels. I need someone who understands what she needs in terms of ovens, prep space, and everything to make it viable."

"El is perfectly capable of doing that."

"Sure, but we want to surprise her for Christmas with the retrofit all done. And whoever designs it has to know the bakery business, but more importantly, know her—how she operates, what she'd like in terms of design. I can handle the colors and stuff, Dad and Trey can handle the mechanical requirements, but I need your expertise for the real guts of the project."

"I'm in. But Dogwood's a small town. How are we going to explain why I've suddenly shown up?"

Dead silence filled the phone . After a long pause, Gio was the first to speak. "We tell her that you and I are a couple again. That'll explain my presence, plus any long gaps in time when she doesn't see either of us."

As uncomfortable as the idea was, he was right. As long as the rest of the family knew it was a ruse, they could keep up appearances in front of Ella.

…and her friends.

…and Annemarie's friends.

…and the townspeople.

He cleared his throat. "But…it won't work if you already have a boyfriend—"

"I don't." She could have kicked herself for how fast she answered him.

"Then it's settled. I can come up this weekend. Can I stay with Trey?"

Annemarie winced. "Um…he's married now."

"Oh." The silence remained as she pondered the obvious answer.

"You can stay in my spare room."

"You sure?"

She repressed a sigh and instead, pasted on a big smile that she knew he couldn't see but might hear. "Absolutely. It'll be fun."

❧ ❧ ❧ ❧

FUN STARTED the moment he got there. With her family all supporting their story of a rekindled romance, everyone managed to camouflage their true mission. Instead, Ella declared that the good news of her sister and her best friend getting together somewhat offset her shattered dreams of owning her own bakery.

The Sinclairs even participated in the subterfuge by pretending they'd hired Gio to help them sell off their equipment. Little did Ella know that many of the sales were actually to her family who planned to integrate the items into Bessy the Bus, now named Bessy's Bus Bites. Trey sketched out several designs, and the family decided on replacing the traditional yellow school bus paint job with one that featured Ella's favorite colors.

"I don't know if it should be pink paw prints on green and white stripes, or green paw prints on pink and white stripes," her mother remarked, studying the two designs Trey had created in those colors. She handed the papers to Annemarie who stared at them, unable to decide.

Gio leaned over her shoulder in order to look at the drawings. At least, that's what she told herself as she was hit with an overwhelmingly familiar feeling that rocked a memory or two...dozen. He turned his head slightly and smiled as if he knew exactly how uncomfortable he made her feel. "What do you think, Annie?" he said softly.

She fought a sudden shiver and pretended to study the two designs, saying the first thing from the top of her head. "Bakeries traditionally use pink boxes, so what if we used a pink and white striped bottom part, border it with green paw prints, and then use the occasional green paw print and green lettering on white for the top half?"

"Perfect," Gio purred in her ear, causing another shiver to shimmy up her spine.

Just then, Ella popped her head in the doorway. "Anybody home?"

Annemarie's first instinct was to pull away from Gio, but he had other plans. As he swept the designs under another stack of more innocuous papers, he reached over and kissed Annemarie. She tried not to flinch, but it took only a moment for shock to turn into something enjoyable.

"I'm just sitting here, complimenting your mom for her excellent taste in daughters," he lied effortlessly. "And I was telling them about a couple of new recipes I've been working on. Want to join me in the kitchen and try some out?"

Ella adopted a knowing smile. "No, but why don't you and Annemarie see what you can cook up? I'll go find Dad. He's probably in the workshop."

Neither Annemarie nor Gio moved until they heard the backdoor slam shut and Ella bellow, "Dad!"

"That was close," Annemarie said with a sigh.

Her mother stood. "Well, it's evident we can't talk about the urprise-say akery-bay uck-tray here."

"Mom, really? Pig Latin?"

Her mother colored slightly. "I get your point. But get mine. Miss Little Bit is a snoop. If she catches just a whiff of our plans, she'll start digging around until she figures everything out."

Gio nodded. "There only one thing we can do. Distract her."

"With what?" Annemarie stared at him, afraid she was reading the answer in his eyes.

"A wedding."

Lydia and Annemarie Handley both gaped at him.

He pretended to study their expressions. "You two have never looked so much alike. This is quite spooky."

"Spooky," Annemarie sputtered. "What about asinine? Ridiculous? Unbeliev—"

"It's genius," her mother stated with a sense of finality. "Absolute genius. We tell her that you want her to plan a reception for a quick wedding on Christmas Eve. Then we turn the tables on her, and instead of a party to celebrate the wedding, we present her with the bus."

"There's no way on God's green earth that she's going to believe that Gio and I are getting married."

Her mother gave her a critical onceover. "Not the way you've been acting lately. You two need to stay at your place more, by yourselves. Take a hike to Bishop's Point to make out."

It was Annemarie's turn to sputter. "Bishop's Point? Mom, I'm not some randy teenager. Trust me, those days are long gone."

Gio wrapped his arm around her. "But you could pretend you were one. For your sister's sake, of course," he added quickly. "I'm game, Mrs. Handley."

"Then Operation: Christmas Surprise is a go."

❧❧❧❧

To her surprise, Ella took the news in stride much too easily. "It's about dang time!" she chortled. "I knew you two were meant for each other the first time I met Gio." She preened around the room. "Match has nothing on me!"

Match! Annamarie thought in panic. *We have to avoid that dog at all costs. If he has an opportunity to match us but doesn't, the jig will be up.*

"The trouble is," she lied, "that I have so much end-of-the-year accounting to complete that I don't have time to arrange anything myself."

"And I'm up to my armpits dealing with the Sinclairs right now," Gio added for emphasis.

Ella put aside her celebration and became all business. "Then let's talk. Simple or elaborate?"

"Simple," the two answered simultaneously.

"Wedding dress, bridesmaids, flower girls?"

"I have a dress, no attendants at all. Just the Justice of the Peace, us, and you and Trey can be the witnesses."

"Super simple, then. And reception?" She turned to Gio. "You'll bake the cake?"

He nodded.

"Then invitations, decorations, dinner—"

"Nothing fancy or expensive." Annemarie searched for a suitable answer that would prevent Ella from making a spectacle out of a pretend wedding. "Maybe a potluck?"

Ella glared at her. "At a wedding? No way. If you want to cheap out, then finger foods."

Gio reached over and placed a kiss on Annemarie's cheek. "The girl is right. We can't cheap out, even if we don't want to make a big to-do about the wedding. People will want to celebrate, and we'll have to feed them something."

Elle found a piece of paper and started scribbling notes. "Then I have to find a location, arrange for music, get a sound system if the venue doesn't have one."

Annemarie squeezed her eyes shut. "I was thinking about the truck bay." When she was met with nothing but silence, she cracked open one eye to see her sister's horrified face.

"You've got to be kidding."

Gio took up the slack. "No, think about it. It's large enough to host practically the whole town, and it's heated. Your father keeps it ridiculously clean. All he'd have to do is move the trucks outside temporarily. You can erect curtains to hide the tool bays. We bring in plank tables, folding chairs, and it becomes a huge reception hall."

"But what about Bessy? There's no way he'd move her out of there. It's the only place where he'll be able to work on her."

"Then we paint her...the wedding colors." He turned to Annemarie with a smile that was almost sincere. "What are the wedding colors, Annie?"

She tried not to choke. "How about white, pink, and green?"

Ella gaped at her. "You? Pink?" She turned to Gio. "Is this what love does to you? Turns you into someone completely different?" She shrugged. "Okay, I'll ask around and see who I can get to slap a coat of paint on Bessy so she won't stick out like a sore thumb." She consulted her phone where she'd been taking notes. "All we lack is a day."

"Christmas Eve," they said together.

Annemarie picked up the narrative. "We could have the reception at three p.m. That's between the end of the two p.m. Christmas Eve service and the five-thirty service so people won't have to choose. Go to the early service then come to the reception. Or come to the reception then go to the later service. Plus there's Bliss's wedding at seven."

"Smart idea. Maybe you haven't completely changed into a pink-loving stranger. So I have enough to start, but you've given me...two whole weeks to perform the impossible. Lucky for you, I specialize in the impossible."

After Ella headed into the other room, Annemarie sank into a nearby chair. "I still think this could blow up in our faces," she whispered. "How do we tell the townspeople that we're really not getting married? There are some people that I trust with keeping a secret, but others..."

"I got this." Gio's smile broadened. "Hey El, one more thing," he called out.

Ella stuck her head into the room. "What?"

"How about we keep the purpose of the party a secret?

We just invite everyone to a Christmas Eve party, and then once they're there, we reveal that we just got married and this is a wedding reception."

"Then it would make more sense to use red and green as the colors. Maybe paint Bessy up like a big Christmas present or something."

Gio appeared to contemplate the idea. "I don't mind having the attendees walk into a place that's not all Christmas colors. We'll have both their attention and their curiosity."

The idea seemed to appeal to Ella. "That's work. I gotta get to work."

❦ ❦ ❦ ❦

To Annemarie's relief, Operation: Christmas Surprise had a smooth start with its official public release. Ella created and sent out a marvelously cryptic but irresistible party invitation and made the arrangements for tables, chairs, food, music, and everything else needed for a Christmas party turned surprise wedding reception turned Christmas surprise. The duties kept her busy and out of Annemarie's hair as well everyone else's as they secretly handled the bus retrofit.

Gio did all the research on the health code regulations they had to follow when designing the bus's interior—what sort of equipment they had to have, and the size and location of the propane tanks necessary to fuel the generator that ran the lights, refrigeration, and the ovens.

"Four sinks?" her father marveled. "That seems excessive for just a bus. Why so many?"

Gio ticked them off on his fingers. "One for handwashing and with a metal barrier between it and the other three. Those are for dishes—to wash, rinse and sanitize. Plus, we need two prep areas—one for human consumption food, and a second one for treats prepared for dogs."

"Live and learn," Annamarie said as she made notations on their working drawings. "Thank heavens the bus is big enough for it all. Oh, I had this idea last night. If we integrate the display case into the service window, people can easily point out what item they want."

Her father pulled out the pencil that he'd tucked behind one ear. "That works. We can also put a removable display case in the smaller window beside the service window." He marked the spot on the plans. "She can opt to use that or take it down, easily."

After two solid days of researching, pricing and planning, they had a functional layout that met all health code regulations. Plus, thanks to the equipment they'd agreed to buy from the Sinclairs, they'd come in under budget, which was very good, because Ella had exceeded her party budget.

"We're not trying to feed everyone a five-course dinner, El," Gio said, studying her proposed menu. "We really need to stick to the budget." He drew an "x" through several items on her list.

"But you only get married once," she complained. "And I want my sister to have the perfect reception, especially since she's not having an elaborate wedding ceremony." She made an admirable job of not pouting.

Annemarie hugged her sister. "I appreciate your efforts, sweetie. But I don't need a lot of frills. Just good food, nice décor, and people I love enjoying the fun with me." She studied Gio's deletions from the list. "I agree with all of these, and you could even cut out the large centerpieces with the fresh flowers and the fairy lights. It's winter. Flowers are going to cost a mint."

"What about silk flowers?" Ella countered.

"If they can be used safely with tea-light candles."

"But we keep the mirror tiles."

"Deal."

Ella sat back as if she'd won the battle that might just win her the war. Smug didn't start to describe the look on her face.

"We've just been had," Annemarie declared to her supposed fiancé. "She knew we'd balk at the fancy stuff, so she made sure to go overboard so we'd agree with her real plan—the silk flowers and tea lights."

"She was like that in school, too." He crossed his arms and pretended to glare at Ella. "Her subterfuge always worked with the instructors."

"But never on you," Ella admitted. "You both knew what I was doing. See?" She grinned. "That's why you're such a great match. You even think alike."

❧ ❧ ❧

As Christmas drew near, the struggle to keep the secrets grew harder. Three different times, Ella almost stumbled across Bessy in mid-retrofit. Luckily, Gio had insisted that they black out the bus's windows to disguise what was going on inside. All she saw was the new paint job on one side of the bus. To their relief, she didn't walk around to the other side where she would have seen the new service window they'd cut into the side of the bus which would have been very hard to explain.

Twice, she tried to weasel the details of the actual ceremony out of Annemarie, but in reality, there were no details to uncover. Realizing she needed to set something up, she went to her preacher and told him all about their nefarious plans.

Rev. Ziegler was the one who came up with the idea that

they should tell Ella they were going to hold the fake wedding at the beginning of the "reception."

"If we can keep her out of earshot," he explained, "I can tell everyone there what is happening. She can think I'm telling everyone that—Surprise!—they're at a wedding. But instead, I'll explain about the new food truck. That way we don't have to pretend I've conducted an actual ceremony." He grew serious for a moment. "The sanctity of marriage shouldn't be trifled with like that." Then his face brightened perceptibly. "But I have no problem with people expecting there's going to be a wedding as opposed to thinking there already was one, then finding out why we've all pulled this stunt."

So, with a slight change in plans, they continued with Gio directing the retrofit per health regulation codes, and Trey and her father doing the actual labor. Annemarie and her mother spent their time distracting Ella and filling her time with plan changes, trips to Denver to get specific décor items ("But I could just order this online...") and anything else they could think of to keep her out of their collective hair.

But she had a way of appearing at the most inconvenient times and places. That included a later-than-usual arrival at Annemarie's apartment where she and Gio were embroiled in making some last-minute adjustments to the equipment layout. Annemarie saw her sister's car pull up and panicked, knowing there was no way they could hide all the papers and schematics in time.

"Ella's coming. What do we do?"

Gio grinned. "I'll take care of it." As he strode to the door, he pulled off his sweatshirt and plowed his hand through his dark hair, tousling it. He stood by the door as Ella rang the doorbell once, then twice. He gestured back at Annemarie to get out of sight and to be quiet. She shifted to the hallway, but had a side view of his face and could hear everything.

He opened the door a crack. "Yeah? Oh hi, El."

She seemed taken aback to see him disheveled and mostly unclothed. "Did I come at a bad time?"

He shifted in pretend discomfort. "Well, actually, yeah."

"Annemarie…"

"Indisposed at the moment. Uh, is there anything you need right now?"

"Well. I—"

"As opposed to something that can wait until morning?" He paused. "Or maybe closer to noon?"

Annemarie couldn't see her sister, but she knew Ella was blushing from the tips of her toes to the tips of her hair. She said something unintelligible.

"Thanks for understanding. See ya tomorrow." As he closed the door, he stifled his laughter as he crossed the room. "That will not only keep her out of our hair tonight, but I bet we won't hear or see her most of tomorrow."

"That was almost mean," Annemarie admitted.

"But totally effective. Not only can we continue what we were doing without being interrupted again, we've sold her once again on the belief that we're solidly on the road to matrimony." He tugged on his shirt. "So where were we?"

Where are we, indeed?

🐾🐾

DESPITE ALL OF THEIR DISTRACTIONS, they hadn't forgotten about the Christmas Cookie Exchange. Ella and her mom took over the rest of the baking, with her mom making cookies for humans, and Ella making some of her famous dog treats. Annemarie made sure to get there in time to help layer the cookies into boxes and load them in her car to take to the church fellowship hall for the event.

Ella held up a label before stocking it on the last box. "I wonder if my Pumpkin Dog Delights logo is too subtle."

"For Mrs. Harrington? Absolutely," Annamarie said. "For anyone else, it's plainly evident that these are dog treats. There's a picture of a dog and the letters D-O-G in large print."

Their mother laughed. "If she gets greedy and sneaks one out of the box without checking, then it's her own fault." She glanced at her watch. "Time to go or we'll be late."

With the car loaded, they drove to the church where eager Boy Scouts waited to help carry in the boxes of cookies. Their mother always prepared a small box that she slipped the boys in thanks for their help. Once inside the church, Annemarie and her family took half of the cookies to the kitchen and laid out the rest of them on the tables in the hall.

The Women's Circle president, Maxine Duff, spelled out the rules in case there were any new participants. She explained that the cookies in the kitchen were being combined to make gift boxes, each with one dozen assorted cookies. Those would be given away to the local police and fire stations for those personnel working over the holidays. They'd also be given to the families of any people incarcerated over the holidays. The rest would be given to the local food bank for families in need, as a festive treat.

Those who made cookies would be able to select from the rest of the many varieties to make their own assorted cookie boxes. Bring six dozen of one type of cookie and you could bring home three dozen assorted cookies.

Annemarie tried to ignore Ella's elbow in her ribs at the sight of Mrs. Harrington maneuvering her way to the front of the line. When the woman picked up one of the dog treats, Ella punched the air with a silent *Hurrah!*

Because of the generosity of the bakers, there were

always cookies left over, even after the selections were made. So the bakers settled down with hot chocolate to sample the remaining cookies. This time, Mrs. Harrington didn't actually eat any of the bone-shaped cookies, so they were spared any drama from her or undue gossip about killer cookies.

But that didn't stop her from gossiping about the mysterious party the Handleys were throwing on Christmas Eve.

"It's really unusual to throw a party on Christmas Eve. So is this a *special* occasion?" Her eyebrows waggled in exaggeration.

Before Lydia could speak, Mrs. Harrington turned to Annemarie. "So who is the handsome man you've been squiring around town? A new flame? Or perhaps an old one?"

Annemarie kept her voice even. "Why, Mrs. Harrington, don't you remember? You met Gio a couple of years ago when you consulted with him about putting in a kitchen in the hotel." Her smile could have curdled milk. "I sure hope your memory isn't going."

The town's second biggest gossip was hanging on the edges of the conversation and took the bait. "Yes, Irene. You have had some mental lapses, recently. I sure hope it's not the first signs—" she looked around with a gleam of conspiracy "—of Old Timer's disease."

Straightening, Mrs. Harrington balanced her fists on her hips. "It's called Alzheimer's, and I'll have you know, Janice Carter, that I'm just as sharp as a tack. In fact…"

Mrs. Harrington and Ms. Carter wandered away, arguing about who was the more mentally aware than the other, both conveniently forgetting about Annemarie, her "squire," and the puzzling party her family was throwing.

"That won't last long," Lydia remarked as the two arguing women melted into the crowd of cookie eaters. "We may have to—" her face folded into a big smile "—toss them some bigger cookie crumbs."

Annemarie wasn't sure who groaned more—her or her sister. But her mother was right. Left on their own, the two biggest gossips in Dogwood could spin a story that would have her anything from getting married, to secretly pregnant, or the long-lost cousin of George Clooney.

"We're going to have to let something slip," her mother said softly, making eye contact with Annemarie. The hidden message: *Think of something!*

But instead of Annemarie, it was Ella with the quick plan. "So we plant the most outrageous stories we can. Like I'm going into the nunnery."

"We're Methodist," her mother stated flatly.

"See? Outrageous." Ella's brow knitted in concentration. "Or that I'm moving away. Or Annemarie's moving away. Or Dad's retiring for real this time."

"Your father has retired three times already."

Ella threw up her hands. "We can't let everyone know we won the mega-bucks jackpot lottery, because our lawyer told us to tell no one," she said in a perfect stage whisper.

The third biggest gossip in town, who had been sitting much too closely, suddenly went pale and got up. They watched her barrel her way through the crowd, evidently in search of Gossips Number One or Two.

Ella dusted off her hands and grinned at her mother and sister. "My job here is done. I think I need another cookie."

Annemarie's mother stared blankly at her departing daughter who skipped blithely away, and turned to Annemarie. "I think I need a drink."

CHRISTMAS EVE CAME MUCH TOO QUICKLY. Annemarie split

her fleeting time on three fronts—keeping Ella away from anything to do with the food truck/bus, battling an influx of friends and neighbors who kept wishing them the best of "luck," and pretending to be in love with Gio.

Operation: Distract Ella required for her to create an absurd set of requirements for the party, many of which had her sister making trips to Colorado Springs and even Denver. Anything to keep her away from the truck bay where her father and brother, along with Gio worked on the bus.

Operation: Distraction Everyone Else wasn't as easy. At first, she thought the "secret wedding" plans had been leaked, judging by the greetings she received, but then when lesser-known well-wishers also offered financial advice, and talked vaguely about start-up loans, business loans, and such, Annemarie realized Ella's lottery story had gained some traction. She kept her replies vague, and if someone asked outright, she answered them honestly. She hadn't won any lottery.

Then there was Operation: Protect Your Heart which Annemarie battled daily and continued to lose. All of her old feelings for Gio had resurfaced with a vengeance, and the differences that had broken up their relationship a couple of years ago now seemed petty and insignificant. That, or both of them had grown up a lot.

Gio sure had. He seemed more thoughtful, more caring. Happier. The moody Italian she remembered had mellowed considerably, and she could only chalk it up to the fact that he was really enjoying his portion of the surprise.

Every night, he came back to her apartment, showered, and then cooked her a magnificent dinner. While they ate, he regaled her with his triumphs in the chore of retrofitting the bus.

"The whole food truck industry is really picking up

across America," he explained while toying with his pasta. "It's economical for a start-up business, and is a good way for an established concern to expand into new territories without sinking capital into a location or a community that might turn out to be a bad fit. It serves areas that might otherwise be a food desert, or only needs temporary food sources, like a job site."

"I'm relieved you're enjoying it. Now I don't feel so guilty for pulling you into this mess."

"Mess? Far from it. I'm fascinated, and I'm learning so much stuff—from your Dad about installation, and from my research into health code and such. This just might be a potential business for me."

As much as she loved his excitement, the little flame of hope inside of her dimmed. With her luck, he'd take his amazing idea and new practical experience back to Denver where he'd turn it into a multi-million dollar company.

And forget all about her.

As it grew closer to Christmas Eve, his sense of accomplishment obviously grew, as did her sense of impending doom. Yet, even if logic told her to stop pining for the impossible, her heart didn't listen.

All I have to do is keep this up for one more day. Then he'll leave, and my life will return back to the everyday mundane.

That evening, after putting up with a steady stream of friends with honest sentiments, strangers with crass requests, and everything in between, she walked into her apartment, turned off her cell phone, and dropped to the couch in an ungainly heap.

"Rough day?" Gio stood in the kitchen door, wiping his hands on the only apron she owned. It looked far better on him.

"If one more person talks to me about money, or luck, or the distribution of wealth, I think I'll scream."

"Then how about a drink and then dinner?"

"I can't go out. I can't take it anymore."

"Who said anything about going out? I made your favorite."

She rose off the couch. "And that's why I'm marrying you, my dear," she quipped. "Every girl needs a personal chef. It smells delicious. Lasagna?"

He nodded. "Made just like you like it."

As she passed by him, she kissed him on the cheek. "I'm getting spoiled by your cooking." *And your company. And your laughter.*

"Is that such a bad idea?"

She stopped, not quite understanding his remark. "To get spoiled? Yeah."

"No, I'm talking about getting married."

Annemarie stood perfectly still, saying nothing.

He ticked off points on his fingers. "One—we really get along well. Two—I adore your family and I think they like me. Three…" His voice trailed off. "Aw, forget about one and two. The important thing is that I adore you. I can't imagine living life without you. All this playing pretend has opened my eyes to what really could be. I love you. And I think, deep in your heart, you love me."

Her heart wedged itself in her throat and she couldn't speak. Finally, she gulped in some air. Was she hallucinating? Was he actually saying the very words she wanted him to say?

"Well?" he prompted.

"We can't…" She trailed off. "It's not the right…" Finally, the right word came to her. "Yes."

"Yes?" He stared at her. "Yes?" he repeated.

She nodded.

Gio picked her up and swung her around, and there was nothing pretend in the kiss they shared. But she pulled away.

"But it's conditional."

His expression faded a bit.

"Don't worry. It's still yes, but not now. Christmas Eve has to be Ella's moment. Her big gift. We can't commandeer her big moment."

"Of course not. We've all worked too hard to make Bus Bites work."

"So, after Christmas?"

"After Christmas," he echoed. Then after a pause, he added, "But not too long after...okay?"

CHRISTMAS EVE ARRIVED, and Annemarie hadn't felt that much excitement since she was a child, expecting Santa Claus to rappel down her chimney and leave her the list of things she'd painstakingly written in her North Pole letter.

The charade went as far as putting on the summery white dress that Ella had proclaimed a suitable wedding dress. It was when her sister was helping with her hair that Annemarie broke the news that they'd decided to "get married" at the reception rather than beforehand in the church.

Instead of being disappointed, Ella seemed elated. "Perfect. That way more people can be a part of the ceremony, and it'll feel like a real wedding."

At three p.m., the repair facility turned party venue was packed. People wandered around, eating food, chatting, and having a good time, despite the lack of information. Bessy the Bus was partially camouflaged by curtains, and a small stage had been set up, using her pink and white striped paint job as a lower backdrop. Other drapes disguised the paw print motif and kept people from viewing it from the backside.

Annemarie, Ella, and their mother were hiding back in the office, ostensibly to hide from the groom. Thanks to security cameras, they could see Gio, Trey, and Doug as they circulated among the crowd, shaking hands and evidently offering whatever explanations they could to stave off curiosity. When she saw Rev. Ziegler on camera, headed back toward the office, a plan that had been making her gut churn with anxiety and anticipation took sudden root.

"Excuse me," she said to Ella and their mother. She ducked out of the office and pulled the preacher over to a dark corner.

"I need some advice, Reverend."

"Sure, Annemarie. How can I help?"

"I think…I know I love him."

The preacher nodded. "I was just talking to Gio. I know he loves you. And you two want to turn this fake marriage into a real one?"

He was too perceptive. "Yes, but this needs to be Ella's day. All of this has been a ruse to give her her dream bakery. I don't want to do anything that will take away from her joy and happiness."

"Do you think admitting that you and Gio are in love will upset her?"

"No. She already thinks it's true. She's thrilled."

"If you admitted how you initially lied to her, but then really fell in love, would it keep her from enjoying this magnificent gift?"

"Of course not."

"Would she think that anything you announced would take away from her happiness?"

"Not really. She already thinks we're getting married."

"Then why not go ahead and do it? Sure, there's the small matter of getting a marriage license, but I know that Effie Lerner is sitting out there next to the judge, and I believe she has a marriage license form in her purse, all filled out except for one signature—yours."

She gaped at him.

He put an arm around her shoulder. "Honey, I've been around a long time, and I know a perfect couple when I see one. I decided to be prepared just in case. Looks like I made the right judgment call. According to Effie, your young man has already signed the license. All we need is your signature and a couple of 'I Do's'. Then we can get on with this shindig and rock your sister's world. Give me a couple of minutes to get all the pertinent players in place."

When Gio walked into the room a few minutes later, he immediately put his arms around her. "I'm so glad we're doing this now," he whispered in her ear.

"Me, too," she responded.

"The preacher has gone to get the judge. He said it'll only be a minute or two. You don't think your family will be disappointed that they didn't attend the wedding?"

She smiled. "No, I think they'll just be happy that we actually tied the knot."

As they stood there in each other's arms, Annemarie heard a scratching noise. She broke contact long enough to open the door to reveal the black and white border collie named Match.

"Really?" Annemarie knelt by the dog. "You're sure, right?"

The dog lifted a paw and placed it on her knee.

"You know this dog?" Gio knelt next to her. "And you're talking to her?" He sounded more amused than skeptical.

"This is Match. She's a sort of legend around here. She sometimes brings couples together. Other times, she validates a relationship."

"And this time...?"

She beamed at him. "We have her approval to get

married."

Gio laughed. "And here I thought I had to ask your father for your hand."

Match looked at Gio and shifted, and her paw touched Gio's knee.

"Thank you, Match," Gio said, ruffling the fur on the dog's head. "I'm glad you approve. And now I'm talking to a dog," he added with a laugh.

A couple of minutes later, Judge Lerner, his wife, and Match acted as the witnesses at what Rev. Ziegler called the fastest wedding in Dogwood history not involving a shotgun.

"Do you, Giovanni Carlo Tanner, take this woman to be your wedded wife, to have and to hold, from this day forward, for better, for worse, for richer, for poorer, in sickness and in health, to love and to cherish, till death do you part?"

Gio's face shined with something that warmed Annemarie to the tips of her toes. "I do."

Rev. Ziegler turned to Annemarie. "Do you, Annemarie June Handley, take this man to be your wedded husband, to have and to hold, from this day forward, for better, for worse, for richer, for poorer, in sickness and in health, to love and to cherish, till death do you part?"

"I do."

"Since there are no rings for the moment, why don't we just skip to the kissing part and then let's get out there and explain to the folks exactly what's really going on?"

They kissed, and whether people liked to call them sky rockets, fireworks or whatever, her head and heart exploded simultaneously in sensations of excitement, fear, anticipation, and outright love. After several minutes, she regained her balance and her sense of time.

"We gotta get out there," she exclaimed.

Gio squeezed her hand. "You get your mom and Ella, and

I'll round up the guys."

When she stepped into the office, her mother took one look at her face, then beamed. The two had never been able to keep secrets from each other, and this was no exception.

"C'mon, Ella. It's time to go," her mother said, grabbing her younger daughter's hand. As she pulled Ella around Annemarie, she gave her oldest a quick kiss. "I saw Match stroll into the office before the judge got there, so I can guess what happened. Good decision, sweetheart. Really good decision."

When they stepped out onto the makeshift stage, her father, brother, and—her throat tightened—her…husband waited for them. Her father commandeered the microphone. By his gleeful expression, she knew he was aware of what had happened in back.

"Ladies and gentlemen, we appreciate you taking time from your Christmas Eve festivities to join us here today. We're here to celebrate two occasions. The first is the marriage of our daughter Annemarie to Gio Tanner."

The crowd reacted in gasps, then cheers and applause.

Ella's initial look of elation faded and she turned to her sister. "Hey wait, you mean you did it already? Without me?"

Annemarie gave her sister a quick hug. "Yes, but be quiet and listen."

Their father continued. "The second occasion has been the best and the hardest secret to keep in my life. It involved everyone in our family with the exception of our youngest, Ella." He turned to grin at her. "As most of you know, she was preparing to purchase Eats & Treats until that deal fell through due to circumstances beyond her control and that of the Sinclairs." He nodded at the couple who sat toward the front of the room.

"But we Handleys are a tough lot. Give us lemons and we'll make lemonade—or, in Ella's case, the best lemon rum raisin cookies you've ever eaten. Give us an old bus, and we'll turn it into something wonderful." He gestured to Annemarie and Gio who took their positions on opposite sides of the stage.

"It's my pleasure to present to you Mr. and Mrs. Gio Tanner and it's their and our pleasure to present to Ella Handley…" He gave the signal and they pulled at the ropes that released the curtains, revealing Bessy the Bus in her entirety.

"Her new mobile bakery truck!"

Applause and laughter filled the air. The bus now sported a green roof, and the sides were pink and white stripes. The window raised up to form an awning, and a counter popped up from the side. The very fairy lights that Annemarie had nixed from the centerpieces now dangled from the awning. The words "Bessy's Bus Bites" were written along the side, punctuated with the occasional dog paw. A trail of paw prints ran down the side of the bus.

Ella screamed, fell to her knees, and then jumped up and ran over to the bus. Then she dashed back to hug her parents, and ran back to the bus, half crying, half screaming the entire way. Gio left his post and took Annemarie's hand, and they followed Ella to the bus.

"Want a grand tour?" he asked Ella.

Ella nodded, her voice now completely gone. He helped her up the steps at the rear of the bus and opened the door to reveal everything she'd need to have a mobile bakery truck. The interior gleamed in stainless steel—twin ovens, an industrial mixer, two refrigerators, two prep spaces, holding racks, a storage space for her bakeware, the triple sink for dishes, the hand-washing station, and more. He gave her the rundown of the equipment, but Annemarie knew her sister was beyond comprehending much more than "Shiny," and "Mine."

She finally regained some ability to speak. "This is why Gio came?"

Trey had joined them and answered her. "Yep, he came for you." Then her brother laughed. "But he's staying for her."

"But the marriage...it's real?"

Gio nodded. "As of about five minutes ago."

"But the plans to get married..."

"It was a ruse to start, so we could keep Bessy a secret. But like Gio said, as of about five minutes ago, it became real."

Her mother gave her youngest one more hug. "We have a lot of people who'd love to see Bessy in all her glory. Think we can share her a little before she becomes your place of business?"

She gulped and nodded and turned to the line forming just outside of the bus.

Gio took Annemarie's hand and they slipped out of the bus, down the line of well-wishers, and ducked behind the remaining curtain.

"I don't know who's more excited, me or Ella," he admitted. "You sure caught me by surprise by agreeing to the ceremony."

"I didn't realize I wanted to get married until you signed the license. Then it all made sense."

"I'm very happy to meet you, Mrs. Tanner." They shared a long kiss that spoke of an even longer future together. After a while, Gio broke away. "Wait, I didn't sign the license yet."

"But Rev. Ziegler told me you did."

"He told me *you* signed the license first."

They pondered the implications for several moments before Gio sighed and tightened his hug. "Does it really matter?"

"Not one bit."

RECIPES

HERE ARE the sugar cookies Lana and Sam made in "The Sugar Cookie Miracle" by Jodi Anderson:

Miracle Sugar Cookies

INGREDIENTS:
> 2 ½ cups flour
> ½ tsp. baking powder
> ¾ tsp. baking soda
> ¾ cups softened butter
> 1 ¼ cups sugar (white)
> 1 egg
> 1 ¼ tsp vanilla extract
> ½ tsp. cinnamon
> Crushed peppermint sticks, to taste

INSTRUCTIONS:
> Preheat your oven to 375 degrees F. Mix together the

flour, baking powder and baking soda in a small bowl. Put aside for the moment.

In a larger bowl, mix the sugar, cinnamon, and butter until creamy smooth. Beat in the vanilla and egg. To this mixture, gradually blend in the dry ingredients.

Scoop the dough into teaspoon-sized amounts and roll into balls. Put onto ungreased cookie sheets.

Bake for 8 to 10 minutes in the preheated oven. Halfway through the baking cycle, sprinkle a small amount of the crushed peppermints onto the top of each cookie, if desired. Continue the original cooking time until the cookies are a light, golden brown.

Let stand 1 - 2 minutes after removing from oven, then place on wire racks to cool.

Enjoy your Miracle Sugar Cookies!

ELLA IS a great baker for people and for dogs. Here are some of her recipes from "Operation: Christmas Surprise" by Laura Hayden:

Mrs. Claus's Buttons

INGREDIENTS:
    2 sticks butter
    ¾ cup granulated sugar
    1 egg yolk
    2 tsp vanilla extract
    1 tsp lemon zest
    2 cups flour
    ½ tsp baking powder

¼ tsp salt
½ cup orange marmalade
Confectioners' sugar

INSTRUCTIONS:

Melt both sticks of butter over medium heat until browned, then cool. Mix with granulated sugar until fluffy. Beat in egg yolk, vanilla, and lemon zest.

In a separate bowl, whisk the flour, baking powder, and salt; stir into the butter mixture, then chill 45 minutes. Scoop into tiny balls and bake 10 to 12 minutes at 325°F. Cool, then split and sandwich marmalade between top and bottom. Dust with confectioners' sugar.

For High Altitudes: reduce baking powder to ¼ tsp, reduce sugar to ½ cup, add 2 tbsp water, and increase oven temp to 350°F.

Pistachio Linzer Cookies

INGREDIENTS:

1 cup shelled pistachios
2/3 cup packed brown sugar, divided
2 cups all-purpose flour
1/2 teaspoon baking powder
1/2 teaspoon salt (1/4 tsp if using salted pistachios)
1 teaspoon orange zest
½ teaspoon grated nutmeg
⅛ teaspoon ground clove
1 cup / 2 sticks unsalted butter, softened to room temperature
1 large egg

2 teaspoons pure vanilla extract

1/2 cup raspberry jam or jelly

Confectioners' sugar, for dusting

INSTRUCTIONS:

Grind the pistachios in a food processor and add 1/3 cup brown sugar.

In a bowl, whisk flour, baking powder, nutmeg, cinnamon, and salt together. In a second, larger bowl, use mixer to beat the butter and remaining brown sugar until creamy. Add the egg and vanilla, and beat until combined.

Add flour mixture and the ground pistachio mixture to the butter/egg/vanilla mixture and mix until combined. It'll start out crumbly, but will come together after a couple of minutes.

Divide the dough into several portions and flatten them out. Wrap in plastic wrap and chill for anywhere from 2 hours to 3 days. You may need to allow chilled dough to warm up before it's pliable enough to use. Preheat oven to 350°F.

Work cookie dough on floured surface and roll until 1/4 inch thick. Cut into 2 inch circles. Cut a smaller "keyhole" circle in half of the circles. These will form the top lid of the layered cookies. The lids will take a bit less time to bake, so put them on their own cookie sheet.

Bake the bottom whole circles for about 10 minutes, (rotating the sheet halfway through) until lightly browned. Bake the lids for 8 minutes (rotating the sheets halfway through). Dust the lids with confectioners' sugar, then put all circles on a wire rack to cool.

Spoon 1⁄2 teaspoon of jam on each bottom, and spread it just shy of the edge. Place a lid on top of the jam and lightly press down to make a cookie sandwich. Dust with confectioners' sugar.

Mrs. Harrington's Pumpkin Peanut Butter Treats (for Dogs, Not Gossipy Women)

INGREDIENTS:

2 1/2 cups whole wheat flour

2 large eggs

15 oz / 1 can of pumpkin puree

3 tablespoons peanut butter (never use PB made with Zylitol—it's bad for dogs. Check your labels, especially on "natural" or low-calorie brands)

Dog-bone-shaped cookie cutter

INSTRUCTIONS:

Preheat your oven to 350°F .

Mix all ingredients together until the dough turns into small balls. If it's dry, you can add a small amount of water. If it's sticky, add a bit of flour.

Use your hands to form a large ball of dough. Roll on floured board/surface until about ¼ inch thick. Use cookie cutter to make bones and place on cookie sheet. The peanut butter will make it pretty easy to remove the cooked cookies from the sheet. Bake for 15-20 minutes for soft treats. Up to 30 minutes for crunchy ones.

Dear Reader,

The seven authors in this series are all in one critique group in Colorado Springs, Colorado. We wanted to write a series together, so we brainstormed a concept at a Romance Writers of America conference. Since we all love animals, we created Dogwood, a special town south of Colorado Springs. No, it's not real, but we wish it was!

And if you enjoyed reading this book, please share your love for the Dogwood Series by leaving a review, even if it's only a sentence or two! Word-of-mouth is vital for an author to succeed. That's how other readers find our books! Your reviews make a ton of difference and are so appreciated.

Monthly Prize Drawing

The series authors will donate goodies to a monthly Dogwood Delights box, including such things as signed books and fun pet-related items. We will draw one name at random from subscribers to our monthly newsletter, the *Dogwood Digest*, so if you want to be considered, sign up at DogwoodSeries.com/monthly-prize-drawing/

Learn More

Visit our Website at DogwoodSeries.com
Join our Facebook Group at
Facebook.com/groups/dogwooddevotee/

And, in appreciation for the work done by animal rescue organizations, each author will donate a portion of all sales to one of them.Thanks for reading!

DOGWOOD SERIES BOOKS

These are in order of publication, but may be read as stand-alones in any order.

A Match in Dogwood, a Dogwood Romance Prequel
Anthology with seven authors

Chasing Bliss, a Dogwood Romantic Comedy
by Jodi Anderson

Sit. Stay. Love., a Dogwood Romantic Comedy
by Pam McCutcheon

Love at First Bark, a Dogwood Sweet Romance
by Jude Willhoff

Must Love Dogs, a Dogwood Sweet Romance
by Karen Fox

Second Chance Ranch, a Dogwood Sweet Romance
by Sharon Silva

A Dogwood Christmas, a Dogwood anthology

Coming Soon:

Doggone, a Dogwood Cozy Mystery
by Laura Hayden

Welcome Home, Soldier, a Dogwood Romance

by Angel Smits

ABOUT THE AUTHORS

Jodi Anderson is the author of romantic comedies, contemporary romances, and dark paranormal fantasy romance. She lives in the foothills of the Colorado Rocky Mountains with her family and one furkid, Bandit, while dreaming of a place called Dogwood. To learn more, visit Jodi's website.

   Karen Fox is the award-winning author of paranormal romance and YA urban fantasy; the Dogwood Series is her first foray into books without a "woo-woo" factor. She works as a Technical Project Specialist for The MITRE Corporation designing web-based applications, and lives in Colorado Springs with her husband, granddaughter, and several cats (the exact number is subject to change). To learn more, visit Karen's website.

Laura Hayden was born and raised in Birmingham, Alabama. The wife of a career military officer, Laura has moved with surprising frequency and practiced efficiency from Alabama to Texas to Virginia to Colorado to

Kansas back to Virginia to North Dakota to Montana, Colorado and finally back to Alabama. Laura now lives in her hometown of Birmingham, where, besides writing, she owns Author, Author! Bookstore. She shares her home with her husband and three rescue dogs: Cooper, Stanley, and Mollie. To learn more, visit Laura's website.

Pam McCutcheon is the author of romantic comedies, fantasy short stories, and nonfiction books for writers under her own name, and the Demon Underground Series as Parker Blue. She lives in Colorado Springs with her rescued Maltese, Daisy, but wishes she could live in Dogwood. To learn more, visit Pam's website.

Sharon Silva is the author of heart-warming romance, romantic suspense, and historical nonfiction. She spent her childhood in the Colorado mountains and fell in love with the magical world of story at an early age. Her works reflect her passion for romantic adventures, the mysteries of ancient spiritual places, and the intriguing possibilities of mystical realms. Sharon enjoys the outdoors and a simpler way of life. Both echo in her writings and make Dogwood her fantasy place to live. She currently resides in Colorado Springs with her husband and their cat, Taz. To learn more, visit Sharon's website.

Angel Smits shares a big yellow house, complete with gingerbread and a porch swing, in Colorado with her husband, daughter, and Maggie, a

Border collie mix. Winning the Romance Writers of America's Golden Heart Award was the highlight of her writing career—until her first book hit the shelves. Her social work background inspires her characters, while improv writing allows her to torture  them. It's a rough job, but someone's got to do it.To learn more, visit Angel's website.

Jude Willhoff is a bestselling author of award-winning books filled with love, laughter, and always a happily ever after. She lives in the mountains of Colorado at the base of Pikes Peak with her beloved husband; their dog Maddie, a mischievous black and white  Chihuahua; and Sheldon, their persnickety orange tabby cat who thinks he's a guard cat. To learn more, visit Jude's website.

Made in the USA
San Bernardino, CA
05 December 2018